I0453054

What Is It Press Copyright 2020
Editor: Sebastian De Angelis
Author: Sue Yan Nish
Series Start Date: 11-26-2013
Revised: 03-17-2020
ISBN: 978-0-9679947-2-7
ASIN: B07D5KDCMB
GGKEY: K0L7QWAD2G6 E

The manual (SM069) is no longer provided in the appendix of the books in the Empty Nation (EN) series because it grew beyond a reasonable size. So it's published separately on Amazon (small cost), Google Play Books (free) and also available for free when you purchase this title on Audible.com, the accompanying PDF support material (SM069) will be available in your Audible Library along with the audio book.

References to Manual are made throughout the books in the series. Tag format: the word being referenced is tagged in **bold** print preceding the reference in square brackets. Reference format: a period [**.**] the dot symbol is used to separate the components of the reference, as in the following examples.

Tag [*section* dot *sub-section* dot *description*]

SIT [4.D-G2.22], section 4, sub-section D-G2, description 22
PBS [2.10], section 2, description 10
SEC [26], section 26

EN01: Breeding

C01 Modern Nation Building: Empty Nation is a, sci-fi, romantic, erotic, political satire, comedy. The story begins two hundred years in the future. In this first book the framework for the entire series is defined. Yanket & Seymour concoct a wild futuristic plan for a new government program, the MSES®, to control the economic fate of the world (nothing new). Note: the appendix for the entire series is in the SM069 Manual available on both Audible.com and Amazon.com websites.

C02 Program: Seymour explores for the first time how absolutely wild their plan really is. Yet supplying a sufficient amount of good-time sex to the workforce is deemed essential to the Nations survival. Yanket & Seymour wrangle with the Cunt-gress to support their MSES® scheme regardless of the social and political nightmare it may cause.

C03 Family: The two main characters in the Series, Mary & Jane (the Gurls) are breed into existence and introduced to the readers and listeners (available on Audible.com). This book steps through a brief history of the Gurls, from conception, birth and breeding by the Human host families. All the while, they're being indoctrinated into the USA Inc. political and economic systems by government supplied drugs to maintain a pleasant and sensual, sedated-state in a surrealistic world as Sex-Slaves (Sissies) for profit.

C04 HCC: This story has many concepts which are bitter & sweet till you realize you're reading fiction. The USA Inc. government in the future is portrayed as an imperialistic, monstrous demon shunned by all other nations and the UN. The society in the new America crosses some pretty taboo moral lines supported completely by the new US second constitution with amendments. So performing lewd sex acts and behavior was legitimizing for citizens in and out of public. And what better way to nullify the old morals of the Caligula type society than through religion. The final scene has Jane Gurl, who is a one year old, baptized at the Holy Cockolic Church (HCC) and her mother goes to confession which requires deep penetration penance.

Books in the Empty Nation (EN) Series

Sissydom Manual (069)
Breeding (1)
Growing Up (2)
The Truth (3)
Careers (4)
Birth (5)
Chosen (6)
Conceive (7)
Monks (8)
Hillary (9)
LA (10)
Disparity (11)
CUNT (12)
WMD (13)
Trumpism (14)
Satan (15)
Queen (16)
Island (17)
Earth (18)
Ur-Anus (19)
(20)
(21)

Empty Nation

A dirty story about a dirty country

Series (1), Book (1)

Breeding

Sue Yan Nish

Table of Contents

EN01: Breeding 2

Chapter: 1 Modern Nation Building...7

Chapter: 2 Program 69

Chapter: 3 Family 107

Chapter: 4 HCC 167

Review Request & Suggestion 203

The Official Sissydom Manual SM069 204

About the Author Sue Yan Nish..207

Words from the Author 208

Author Contact Info..210

Chapter: 1 Modern Nation Building

The year is, 2222...

[1.1] PREPARATION

Aaaagh! Oooh! Honey, you're best! Ahhh! Kisss... The best I've ever had. Humm... Kissss... All of you are good, but none as good as you Tammy.

Gak, Gulb, Guk, Guk, Guk... Ooooh... Hank, I love you so much sweetheart! Kisss... kiss...... (With her husband's manhood lodge deep into her throat, Tammy swallows the copious amounts of sperm wads afterwards, as any devoted Whore-Wife would do, she slowly retracts his lengthy cum-hose, cleans her man's shaft and respectfully kisses the tip of it). Ummm... Yummy! Yummy! Your Jizzzies taste soooo... good Baby, kisss... Mwah... Anything for you Baby! Mwah... Mwah...

Hmmm.... Kiss... Kisss... Hmm... **Honey-Puss**! Why don't you put together training session for the other wives? Show all the gals how you use your magical talented tongue and mouth? I mean, you're a master cock-sucker! Oh! And invite my secretary Nora. She is nowhere near as good as you Honey. Mwah...

Mwah... Thanks Babe! And sure, sure **Hank**, you know I love showing off my talents. To be honest my Mom taught me everything I know about Cock-Sucking. Mommy's a Whore-Wife. She was the one who taught me how to be a good Girl.

Yeah **Tammy**! Your horny family is so sexually liberated. After you shared them with me, I had no doubt in my mind about marrying you into my harem of wives. Mwah...

Thanks Baby! Mwah… Of course, I'll invite all the bitches you're banging on-the-side and all the wives. And I agree **Hank**. All the wives should be able to give you what you need. I'll setup a deep-throat fellatio training session with, Sherry, Tony, Cathy, Sue and Lisa.

Great Honey Mwah… Sounds like a plan. Oh! Look at the time?

Shhh….it… !!!…

It's show time. **Tammy**, I gotta give this speech to a bunch of sociopathic morons. It makes me wonder how universities can handout Mind Control degrees to such cognitively challenged individuals.

Oh **Hanky**, you carry the weight of the world on your shoulders, Mwah… I love you Sweetheart (Tammy sighs and drapes herself over her husband). Mwah…

Tammy Honey, you and all the wives are always on my mind. I get a tingling sensation in my balls every time I think of you girls. Mwah… Love you too… Mwah… Hey! What are we having for dinner tonight?

Oh it's Tuesday, so it's Cathy's night to cook and she usually makes a, Stud-Grade, **FEMA** [4.D-G7.13] camp, mystery meat dish.

Uuugh! Damn it! Not human meat again! Honey, why don't you stop at the Chinese imported gourmet food store on the way home and pick us up some non-human meat.

Yeah sure **Hank**, the Chinese food store always has the freshest food in town. It's way better than any of the contaminated reconstituted American crap. Kisss...

Oh yeah, for sure **Tammy** lover! Mwah… And as the director of the Department of Health and Mind Control, the **DHMC** [4.D-G6.1] I can afford to eat imported food from China. It's not a crime for a government official and his family to **not** eat what's offered to the masses.

Definitely **Hank** Honey! Besides the American **GMO** crap will kill you!

Oh yeah Tammy, the **Mon-Satan-O** [4.D-G1.19] GMO shit causes deceases! Not to mention the patented-seed enslavement of farmers. Makes me wonder how the American government veered, so far off the path of caring for its citizens! Where did we go wrong?

Honey, I'm a Bimbo! I don't know stuff like that Sweetheart. But **Hank** Baby, you're the kindest man I ever put-out for. Our Corporatocracy politicians here in the USA Inc. worship money not life. And you're so generous to me and the other wives. Cock is the new money! Win-Win Baby! I love you so much... ummm… Kisss...

Kisss... Love you too Honey-Bunny, kisss... Our predecessors, from the Clitcum, Boosh, OBomb and Tramp era, the **CBOT** [21.B.5] era sealed the fate of the working class in America. The USA Inc. will never fall back into a charitable Cunt-trie ever again. The USA Inc. follows Platonism, the wealthy rule and everyone else is a slave.

Ooooooh **Hanky**! Mwah… Yes! Elites rule the world now! And, and you're such a big part of it in several ways (Tammy is on her knees holding her husband and slaps her face with it to prove her point about her reference to big). You're sooo long and smart sweetheart! Mwah… (Tammy lavishes her benefactor with praise while squashing her enormous tits in his face).

Well Tammy, you might be one of the dumbest Girls I ever married, but you're right Sweetheart, nothing changed after the revolution of 2169. And that Jackass President Donald **Tramp** [23.39] didn't really help matters. But actually they're all war criminals, the Demo-Cunts, Repubic-Cunts. Plato would have loved the arrogance of Tramp the white supremacist.

Mwah… Oooooh! I get soooo turned-on when you start talking world domination stuff to me! Mwah… (Tammy furiously starts fingering herself). Yeah! Ahhhh…

Down Girl, down… Kisss… **Tammy** you have an insatiable appetite for sex! You're always turned-on Baby! Mwah… Kisss… Might have to go a second round here. Mwah… (Hank unzips his pants and pulls out his limp dick which hangs down almost to his knee cap).

Oh my! Your sooo long Baby! It always reminds me of the time My Mom and I performed with an erotic circus troupe. Our act was called, the Amazing Snake-Girls!

Wow Tammy! You're a very talented Girl. Mwah… Here swallow this (Hank twirls his penis at Tammy as if it was a jump rope).

Oh Honey! You're so generous to me and to all the wives. Mwah… yeah, Guk, Gak… I can swallow any man like a python! Ahhh… I learned how to be a Cock-Swallower, a good-girl from the reptiles in the erotic circus! Guk, Gak…Glrglk…

Mwah… Yeah! Swallow it like snake bitch! Ahhh… Ooooh! You're a Snake-Girl. No one can swallow like you! Ahhh… And **Tammy**, I like to give my Girls what they need. (Hank pushes his lengthy manhood down his wifes eager and wide-open mouth). Yeah Baby! Ahhhh… The whole fucking thing Baby! Ahhhh…. Yeah…

Guk, Guk, Gak… (Tammy swallows the entire snake of a cock then quickly regurgitates it out to say something). Love you Hank with all my heart and pussy! Kisss...

Love you too Baby! Mwah… And I have no idea how you get the entire length of my dick down your throat! Huh! I mean wow, this is why I want you to train the other wives.

Sure I'll train the Girls to use their throat muscles to take your magnificent man muscle. Mwah…

But Babe, sometimes those bad people, the Demo-Cunt, Repubic-Cunt politicians they do things right? Nasty bad things, right? (Tammy says in a fearful voice). And my Lady Friends and I were in bed playing with our pussy and they said things I think I shouldn't have heard.

Things about their pussies? (Hank says inquisitively, want to hear a juicy story).

No Baby! We all love eating each other's pussy! I heard things. Bad, bad things. As a women owned by a man, I don't think I was supposed to hear things like that. Mwah… (Tammy smooches her husband while lifting his fat wallet out of his pants). Mwah… I feel so dirty Baby! Mwah…

Haaaa haaa ha! Its okay, it's okay. Mwah… Ahhh, just tell me what you hear sugar-puss? What did the bad Girls tell you? Kisss…

Naughty bad thing **Hanky**, Snifff… Snifff… (Tammy turns on the tear faucets to gain Hanks sympathy). Spank me Baby! I'm a bad Girl!

And yes, I give you permission to pick my pocket, but you know the rules, you sweet little slut. If you want money you have to work for it, like every other whore wife I have.

Mwah… Mwah… (Tammy immediately gets on her knees and kisses the tip of her master's instrument of pleasure). Well **Hanky**, they say if it wasn't for soybeans and human meat mixed together to make FEMA spam, the American population would starve. I don't think much and don't really want to, but I was told to consider this to be very logical!

Really? Hmmm… Human body parts? Ahhh… Where's the logic? Enlighten me **Tammy**!

Well **Hank** Baby, the Girls told me we're smart here in the USA Inc. We control our population size the intelligent way.

Intelligent? Wow! You're scaring me. How are we controlling the savages, **Tammy**? (Dr. Yanket is actually still sane at this point in the EN series).

Mwah… **Hank**, by elimination of the non-conformist members of society! They're not useful anymore! So we use them as feed for the productive ones. And I hear that they all have really small dicks, so they're totally useless to a hyper-sexual pussy Lady like me!

Haaa haa ha, again **Tammy**, Where do you cum up with this shhh…it? Which whores are you hanging-out with?

Hank, I'm a sexy Bimbo-Girl with needs (Tammy to exhibit her needs, lifts up her top and fondles her monster set of tits that Hank bought for her). Huh! Honey, I have zero original thoughts in my head, but I was told to just think it's serendipitous we have so many detainees in FEMA camps to process into food for the patriotic Americans who comply with the Standard Submissive Behavior, the **SSB** [4.D-G2.30] laws.

Huh (Hank sighs) Yeah your tits cost so much I consider them a financial asset. And yeah I guess you're right, workers have to eat something (Hanks feeling-up Tammy). They are fucking big!

Agh! **Hank** (This wife is obviously a psychopathic with zero empathy for anyone outside of her immediate circle of cunt-munching girlfriends). Kisss… Mwah… Ooooh Baby…

Oh for sure **Honey**. I mean most American's are in FEMA camps nowadays because they're too smart for their own good! They think too much like your whore friends!

I totally agree with you **Hanky**! Thinking is a waste of time, for anyone. Mwah… Guk, Guk, Gak… (Wanting to prove she's a good girl, Tammy slides her man's entire thing back down her throat again). Guk, Guk, Gak… Glrglk…

Ahhhh… Right! Haaa ha… Who told them they can think! It's ridiculous! Hey gotta go Babe! Speech time! Kisss... kiss... see you home **Tammy**.

Guk, Guk, Gak… (She pulls it out with ease). Honey, love you **Hank**... Hmmm.... kiss... kiss, I adore you! I worship your cock, I mean you, I worship you and your money! Mwah… Mwah…

Tammy, Love you too sweetheart. Kiss all the wives for me. I'll be home around six tonight.

[1.2] THE SPEECH

Gentlemen, distinguish members of the National Association of Mind Control (NAMC) and to all the uninvited, but somehow wormed their way into the meeting anyway, Trilateral Cum Mission, **TLC** [23.49] members. Welcome to the annual Domination Conference.

Applause... Applause... Applause... (Lots of clapping). Go Hank!

The Conference is sponsored by the **DHMC** [4.D-G6.1] and the USA Inc. Office of Special Cunt-Sell, the **OSC** [23.51].

Applause... Applause... Applause... Hanky! (Shouts a large breasted woman from the crowd). Wink, wink (She then blows Hank an air-kiss while she opens her trench coat exposing her naked body to him). Kiss… kisss…

Huh, Okay, wink, wink, Kisss… (Hank never being one who turns down an offer from a beautiful lady, winks and air-kisses back). The OSC is looking into the gross mismanagement of penis in the USA Inc. The disappearance of our labor force is being associated to the reduction of cognitive able caused by the decrease in penis size of the American male workers.

Applause... Applause... Applause...

Thank you, thank you... The OSC investigation will determine whether we are a nation of men or pussies. But here at the conference we will focus on economic inequality regardless of penis size.

Applause... Applause... (Clapping from the crowd).

At no time in the history of the United States has there been a larger inequality gap between the haves and have-nots. This economic disparity has caused a dilemma for our countries government. It now needs the full cooperation of its downtrodden citizenry it created through penis shrinkage. So the oppressed and unemployed are ignoring our government's pleas.

Booo… Booo…Boooo… Cocks rule!

I hear you! But their masculinity was fooled with. I'd be pissed-off if someone besides my wives missed with my Willie. So they're rightfully upset. Workers are basically telling their government to go screw-off!

Grumble, grumble, grummm... (The wealthy Stud crowd has zero empathy for the poor in this new society).

Yes, I hear you! But and you and I both know why workers are pissed-off! I'm not gonna try and sugar-coat this problem and tell you some bullshit story about being the greatest nation on Earth. When the reality is, it **WAS** a great nation! This is a Cunt-trie trying to be what it was, just look at its history.

We all know this wealth gap between our citizens started when the old US government's Neo-Fascist oligarchy had gutted the entire working middle-class from its workforce. They did this by first going off the Bretton Woods system. And then Cunt-gress passed trade agreements like NAFTA, TPP, TIPP and raised corporate taxes plus trade tariffs which encouraged US businesses to outsource American jobs to foreign countries.

Grumble, grumble... Grumble grmm... Fascism is the new Democracy! Grumble…

Right! This same corrupt psychotic government bankrupted the US Treasury by allowing a private banking cartel, the Federal Reserve, to dominate its money system for several hundred years, rendering the once strong gold backed US dollar into a worthless fiat piece-of-crap currency.

Grumble, grumble, hmmm… grummm... (This irritated elite group of wealthy businessmen is funded by the very thing Hank is putting a negative spin on).

Please, let me finish! Then adding insult to injury our fascist government in **Washingcum** has pissed-off every nation on earth with its imperialistic war machine. We have covertly overthrown every government who wasn't armed with nuclear weapons. Using the guise of democracy we've raped and pillaging everything in our path.

Hmmm… grummm... (The NAMC dudes are scratching their balls wondering why Hanks bashing the USA Inc.).

Wait, I'll elaborate on that! The United States of America was founded on the principles of freedom and justice for all. And it was not our founding fathers intent when crafting the US Constitution to allow a fascist police-state to rise to power. Our government is still run by corporate thugs not elected officials. But as always history repeats itself and the United States has contorted into the same dysfunctional imploding condition the Roman Empire had prior to its fall.

Grumble, grumble… Hmmm… grummm... We're in business! Yeah! The Police-State keeps us stuff safe! Grumble, grumble… (The crowd is a big murmur of opinions whether to metaphorically stone Hank or just walkout on the meeting).

Wait, wait… There is good news though! Tuff crowd (Hank says to himself wondering if he'll be lynched by this mob).

Haaaaa... haaaa.... ha, Haaa.... YOU'RE KIDDING? Grumble, grumble… news my ASS…!!!... (From the heckling, Yanket realizes he has some convincing to do with this group).

Ah yes, I can see some of you laughing. And I realize the thought of any good out cum at this point is hilarious. But the good news is, with the recent scientific discoveries made by scientist and engineers. Who our military has captured, kidnapped or interned. These brilliant minds possess the answers to our future. Here in the USA Inc. we could see a New

Industrial Rebirth. As China had raisin to become the global power, we too will rise again!

Applause... Applause... Applause... (Hank whips the sweat off his brow when he hears the crowd cum back to a positive response).

Well cumed news indeed! With the exception, as I've mentioned, our Cunt-tries well-trained and highly educated workforce, no longer exists. The workforce we need to take advantage of the many new opportunities which could take place due to the game-changing new inventions in, space propulsion, transportation, energy production and material science.

Clap, clap, clap… Applause…

Not only was the productive workforce destroyed by American corporate greed, student loans and drops in college enrollment. But also by the willingness of the American people as a whole, to participate in the US economy or interaction with its own government.

Grumble, grumble, hmmm… grumm... grmm...

This is due to the fact, to our Neo-Fascist government here in the USA Inc. has taken everything cashable from its middle and lower working class citizens.

What's the problem with taking shhh…it. Grumble, grumble… Some win, some loss! Get over it! Yeah! Donald **Tramp** [23.39] showed us how to take shhh…it. Grumble, grumble… (The crowd gets on their feet and pushes towards the stage).

Whoa! Whoa! Wait a minute! We have epic problems with our workforce! Gone are the jobs, the social mobility or any hopes and dreams of a better future. The working class in the USA Inc.

economy which makes up 96.9 percent of the population was eradicated by Casino Bankers in the decades preceding and after the **Financial Holocaust of 2007** [23.5.1].

Grumble, grumble… We don't give a rats-ass Hank! We take what we want man! Yeah! Yeah! Who the-freak are you! Grumble, grumble…

Shut-Up…!!!…

Just shut-up! And listen for once in your miserable lives! The last nail was driven down years ago into the coffin of the US working class. The labor force participation rate of the American worker has been completely beaten down into non-existence.

Grumble, grumble (The crowd, who are all government sponsored or privately funded, are starting to get really perturbed about the bashing of their rights to abuse whom ever gets in their pillaging way).

Right, right, it's absurd I know! But this has all been by the hands of our own government. Our economic down-fall has been through, over taxation, laws, rules, internment, free trade agreements, regulation, tariffs, licensing, debt-peonage and controls generated by our government. This eventually led to a population enslaved, abject poverty and ultimately disintegrated its financial, industrial and research ability as a nation. And this may benefit this NAMC group!

Applause…Applause… Applause… Hank! We don't…

Give a Shit…!!!…

Hmmm… And you wonder why we had a second revolution?

Okay **Nora** bring out the Girls and hey open your blouse, let those huge nobs of yours show. I seriously need a distraction with these assholes (Nora is Hank's secretary).

Wheet Whoo… Applause... Applause... Applause... Wheet Whoo… Yeah! I wanna see it all! Take it off! (The crowd is whistling at the sexy Show-Girls Hank has on the stage. But by now they don't know why-the-fuck they're applauding for).

Yeah! I know what you really want! Okay ladies, take it off, take-it all off! (Some of the Show-Girls, who can't wait, start stripping then toss their lingerie out into the crowd of horny men while Hank takes a bow).

Wheet Whoo… Hey! I know you want me Bitch! Applause... Wheet Whoo… (These heckling guys are all wound-up doing, catcalls, rubbing their dicks and licking their lips at the glorious Girls parading around the stage). Wheet Whoo… Hey Girl, give me smile! You gotta boyfriend? Nice ass…!!!...

I'll continue, this lack of a workforce has made our corporate bought and controlled government start to concoct new ways of getting or I'm sorry, more accurately, **exploiting** the US population to be manipulated under its control again in hopes of molding it into the once productive workforce it had been. Sadly, I just described Neo-Feudalism!

Wheet Whoo… Applause... We're with you Hank! (The men in the crowd are all masturbating to the sight of the scantily dressed Show-Girls who are wearing revealing sexy **Victoria Secretions**® [10.7] lingerie or fancy sequin mini-dresses as they do an erotic dance on the stage next to Hank).

Thank you. Thank you. Yeah, you like what you see, don't you! Yeah! Hank knows what you want!

Wheet Whoo… Applause... Applause... Applause... (The whole crowd has their dicks out and is wolf-whistling at the near naked Show-Girls). Wheet Whoo… Wheet Whoo…

But how can our self-serving, lying, cheating, stealing, ten pounds of democracy crap in a five pound fascist bag government do this? Haaa haa... Well folks, here's a little news for you. Our Cunt-trie has been **BANKRUPT** for centuries. Its natural resources depleted or sold to the Eurasian Nations. The workforce participation rate is zero. And I'm not sure it has anything to do with the size of our dicks in America!

Applause... Applause... I'm large enough! Big is better! My freaken dick is huge bro! Yeah! We don't give-a-shit if workers have small dicks! Yeah! (The chauvinistic crowd shouts).

Haa haaa… very good! Right, right, you're all proud of your Manhood! And that might be all well and good. But most of our professionals, scientists and engineers have all moved to China or California which was surrendered to China as war reparation. In other words, like I said, the United States destroyed itself through its own idiocy, hypocrisy and greed by selling our Cunt-trie to the private banks of the Federal Reserve banking cartel on December 23, 1913.

Grumm Grumble, grumble, grumm... grumm... Fuck-the-Fed, we want the Girls!

And I want you all to know I'm using the word, **government** loosely here. Due to the fact the United States gave up its rights to be a government when it signed away its control of its money supply with the passing of the Federal Reserve Act on a fate-less December day in 1913. Ironically it was the eve, of the eve, of Christmas!

Gentlemen, if you haven't presumed you're screwed yet, you're probably wondering why I'm here today. And although I may speak ill of our post-revolution, struggling government, as loyal Neo-Communist Americans we need to cum up with new ways to control and exploit the US population. Through control of its thoughts we can and must be cum a strong imperialistic nation again!

Applause... Applause... Clap, Clap, Clap... Yeah Hank!

I can promise you this. It's going to be difficult. We've treated our population here in the USA Inc. like animals while the money lenders, politicians and some of you profited. Some say our penis size is shrinking because of the lack of opportunity here in the USA Inc. Some say the government tainted the water supply which could the shrinkage. But regardless of why, this is where you, the academic and research Cum-munities cum into play.

Yah! Applause... Yah! Applause... Applause... We want free shhh...it Hank! Whooohooo... Wheet Whoo... Nice legs! Hey Beautiful! (More heckling and cheesy catcalls).

The Grant proposal...

So let's move on! To encourage you I'm glad to announce the, US Department of Health and Mind Control, the DHMC, is offering a substantial grant award for the institute, university or research group who submits a applicable plan not a pie in the sky scheme. The plan must be, unique, workable and a plausible plan for solving our predicament of having a zero-workforce participation rate.

Clap, Clap, Applause... Applause... (Cheers from the crowd who are taking-turns humping the Whores Hank used to distract them from committing violence acts against him).

And just a note here, your new unique ingenious plans cannot and must not include anyone incarcerated. This includes the use of State and Federal prisons or the Feminizing, Emasculation, Modification Agency, **FEMA** [4.D-G7.13] camp populations. You all know the prison population makes up 69 percent of the US population. And this is mainly due to the prisoners, oh I'm sorry, *yet-to-be*, and possibly never prosecuted detainees, are currently being used by the US Department of Labor as a temporary solution to the labor shortage.

Grumble, grumble, grummm... Grumble... Where we gonna get test subject! Grumble, grumble.

Now, now, calm-down. I hear the grumbling in the crowd because of the elimination of 69 percent of the USA Inc. population who is incarcerated or detained in the FEMA internment camps, or US Private Prison Industry, in the **APPS** [4.D-G2.25.2] system from the equation.

Now let me put all this to rest right here and now, once and for all. I'll reminding you social scientists the 69 percent of Americans who got put in private prison or camps were put there because they were part of a money grab by the private prison industrial complex.

Grumble, grumble, How we gonna fix dysfunctional shhh...it? Grumm... grummm... Grumble (These businessmen have no idea or want to fix there cash-cow private prison system).

And also because they were, affiliated, associated, dues paying members of or had one or more of the following attributes and or conditions, fake news announcers, gun-toting accountants, money-whoring bankers, priests, Nuns, tax evaders, professional wrestlers, constitutionalist, doomsday preppers, managers, professors, truck drivers, lawless corrupt American politicians, teachers, ballot casting voters, Washingcum lobbyists, ex-military, proctologist, erotica story writers, engineers, nose-picking video-gamers, hackers, government beneficiaries, wacked-out scientists, domestic terrorists, United States civil servants, psychologists, construction workers, computer programmers, administrators, back-stabbing lawyers, paid-off Judges, critical thinkers, sport-fans, machinists, conspiracy nuts and capitalists, to name just a few.

Clink! Boom! Clink! (The audience is turning into a mob, throwing bottles and Champaign glasses at the stage). Grumble, grumble…

Whoa! Hey! Watch it! I'm gonna finish with this, just calm down! Look, I know you think this will dip into your profits, so I have a plan!

Grumble, grumble… We need free shhh…it Hank! Screw your bullshit plan! Grumble, grumble… Yeah! Girls! We need Girls!

Hey! I'm one of you. I profit from government abuse of the under-privileged population. It's our bread-n-butter! So be grateful! Seriously be VERY! VERY! Grateful the group was removed from the equation. It's for your own GOOD! Oh yeah, and like I said, the hordes of detainees are currently being exploited by your government, which makes me wonder why they were put in jail in the first place considering I just described most of my friends and family.

Clink! Boom! Clink! Applause... Get the fuck out of here Hank! Girls, Whooohooo… Applause... Boom! Clink! (The disorderly crowd has be cum rowdy. Bottles flying everywhere, a fist fight breaks out over a Show-Girl).

Thank you all... And may your dick sizes increase and the best plan wins! Thank you! Good luck with your grant proposals.

Whoa! Shoot! (Hank tries to make a quick exit and has to duck out of the way of a beer bottle hurdled at him). Tough room!

[1.3] THE DHMC

Oh God! I've done this speech so many times. I'm lucky I got out alive. It gets wider and wider every time.

Sorry to hear that Sir. (Hank's assistant says).

And no matter how much I pump-up the image of the USA Inc. government, it still sounds sinister! Making it sound like our arrogant sociopathic yet benevolent government is, by some weird twist of fate, both loving and caring. This is always a tough sale to make!

Benevolent Sir? (The assistant says).

Huh.... Yeah benevolent my ass, it's our evil warlord master yet somehow I still have to make it sound like our government deserves our cooperation. Huh! I don't know what to do. There's never a good viable, useable response as how to solve our Nations labor force erosion and non-participation.

Ahhh huh! I'm sorry to hear about the erosion Sir, but it is the new norm Dr. **Yanket**.

Wait, yeah, yeah **Son**, the new norm, right. It's not eroding, it's gone! There's no workforce! The bankers are in control of every sector, branch of government and has screwed the US citizens so many times, no one is even listening or believes there's a government or for that matter a currency anymore.

Well **Sir**, after the Petro-Dollar died, we couldn't print any more funny money. So we had nothing of value to pay workers with.

Right **Son**, after the total collapse of the Petro-Dollar, people don't even think it's a government anymore. It turned into a corporation, the United States of America Incorporated.

Yes Dr. **Yanket**, the USA Inc.

Oh and besides how broke our country is, our government is still kicking its citizens in the balls by its vicious militarized surveillance police-state. The military is in the streets alongside the heavily armed law-enforcement which are controlled by Homeland Insecurity. We're killing and imprisoning our population like dogs. And the Transgender Security Administration the **TSA** [4.D-G6.10] conducting penis erection measurements at check-points, isn't helping!

True Dr. **Yanket**, the TSA groped my balls on the way here today.

Well **Son**, I actually like having my balls massaged, I'll talk to you later about that. But you're right. Privacy is a thing of the past. And there're food shortages, the unemployment rate is 69 percent, and the Cunt-Stitution we once had is ignored.

Yes Dr. **Yanket**. I agree.

Patriotism doesn't exist. On top of that the government has confiscated all the gold, silver, condoms, fire arms and paper currency years ago. Okay the private central bankers won! There's nothing left to govern. It's a zoo! Uuugh! We've be cum a Nation of caged animals. The only ones working are the immigrants holding a very limited temporary USA Inc. residency.

[1.4] SUGGESTION

Seymour presents his case…

What are we gonna do **Son**? (Yanket has his head in his hands).

SEX! This is the answer Sir? It's the only resource we haven't explored yet. It's something everyone wants in abundance, especially the impoverished, horny, unemployed American male population, (Said a lowly research assistant from a dimly light corner of the room at the DHMC).

What?

Sir let's give the male population who are willing to work lots of sex. It would make the workforce grow and be productive again.

Yeah, yeah, I think it's a great idea, you IDIOT! As much sex as humanly possible is your answer! Who-the-fuck hired you?

You did Sir.

Oh, oh, well, hey I'm out of answers, so, any answer is better than none!

Yes Sir.

Okay smartass, where're we gonna get the amount of women necessary to supply this much free cunt? No one can afford birth control any more even if it was available. Let's face it, women aren't putting out pussy like they used too!

Because Dr. Yanket there's no contraception available? And the Chinese trade Sanctions against the USA Inc. doesn't help. They make more of the pharmaceuticals in the world.

Yeah not even condoms! Our Fascists Big-Brother government screwed-up the relationship with the Chinese. People are out buying groceries with what little money they do have. And you can't eat expensive smuggled in contraception.

Well I saw a chick swallow the Jizz out of a used condom once!

Yuck! I guess that could be considered of a protein snack!

Haaa haa ha…. I guess, depending on which way you swing!

But having more sex would be more fun! Hmmm… Maybe if folks skipped a few meals and bought contracep… (Yanket ponders like sexual benefit). Hmmm... Geeez! Everything is so messed up! (He then realizes how absurd it sounds). I can't believe the thoughts in my own head anymore!

Yes, but no more delusional than most **Sir**. Things are bad now!

Hell the one thing I do believe is… is... (Yanket, pauses to regain a normal thought, confounded by the complexity of the scheme covers his face with his hands).

What's that Sir?

Ever since the **Financial Crisis of 2007-2008** [23.5.1], family life in America has eroded down to the point where the US population has been decreasing in size for centuries. No one is getting married or having kids anymore. The US has the lowest birth rate in the world. Hell, the mostly unemployed male population can't afford to start families never mind maintain a sexual relationship. Knocking up a bitch is out of the question.

Yes Sir, I totally agree with you!

Well let's face it son, America was once an empire but now it's a third world piece of shit country. The crime rate for rape is at an all-time high, we have the lowest literacy and mortality rates in the world and most folks only have a third grade education. Women all pack illegal guns for protection; it's the Wild West all over again!

Yeah, my point exactly Sir, they're unequivocally horny as can be and disparate for any sex they can get, they'll do anything to get laid! It's so bad most men in the US screw their mother, hell they even poke their grandmother, Uuuooooogh, nasty!

My friend its monkey see, monkey do, and metaphorically the US government would screw its own mother for money so why shouldn't the American citizens?

Yes Sir, I'm with you, the moral fiber which held this country together for centuries is gone. The American exceptionalism based on morally correct, democracy promoting has turned into a fascist empire building imperialistic war-machine cloaked as democracy.

It's true son, I'm glad we're on the same page. You have my ear, what's your solution?

Sir one of my solutions, (said the sheepish research assistant), let's employ men to bend over and take it up the ass.

WHAT? It's crazy, (said Dr. Yanket), promote homosexuality?

Ahhh… Not exactly **Sir**, (Seymour cringes at the response).

And anyway where're you gonna get all the millions of queers needed to do it? I know gay marriage is legal now and everything but we're talking about an army of male cock-whores.

Sir, I seriously wouldn't use defamatory slang, slur phrases or words like queer, fag, pansy, anal assassin, cockpipe cosmonaut, fairy, homo, princess, queen, butt pirate, sausage jockey, sissy, flower, etc…

Sure, sure **Seymour**. Just between us, I have a lot of gay-friend!

And all my wives have gay friends, hell they're all cunt munching whore!

Ahhh… Haaaa haaa… Okay. **Sir**, sorry to interject here but, having gay-friends doesn't mean you're not homophobic. It doesn't justify prejudice.

I know that! Pssss… But hey! They don't get offended when I call them queer. **Seymour** my gay friends love me, not grab my ass love, but you know…Ahhhh… Buddy love. Ahhh… (Yanket goes into a doubtful moment where he questions his sexual orientation). I mean, blow-jobs isn't Gay-Sex, we just share protein snacks! I'm not Gay! I have six wives.

Huh! (Seymour smiles and can't believe he just heard his boss confess his bisexuality to him). Well, maybe so **Sir**, although they say men who make sexist jokes are probably just insecure about their masculinity.

Yeah **Son**, I know I'm sexist asshole, most men are! Look, but I'm trying to change my lifestyle. I'm trying to expose myself to guys more. Look, look, (Yanket unzips is pants and reaches deep into his pants to yank out his long flaccid snake).

Whoa! Okay Dr. **Yanket**, thank you. Wow, you got quite a long man tool there, Sir (Seymour also being a closet bisexual is in total admiration of what he just got a glimpse at).

Yeah **Seymour**, my gay-friends love when I whip it out.

Good for you! But **Sir**, I think you might be using your sexist anti-gay humor to reaffirm your own sense-of-self, particularly when you feel you're masculinity is being threatened.

Okay… (Yanket reluctantly puts his dick back in his pants). What do you suggest **Seymour**?

Well yeah **Sir**, they're friends of yours so you can say whatever you want. However in public I would suggest toning-it-down a bit. We wanna make statements to the press which are, politically and or socially correct with no malicious intent insinuated.

Yeah, yeah… I hear you. Huh! You know **Seymour**. It's kinda funny, no actually ironic. The USA Inc. is now the lease sexually liberal Cunt-trie in the world.

Yep! You're right **Sir**. American Exceptionalism movement, the **AEM** [23.15b] became exceptions to our freedom. The movement has been linked to the American Oedipus complex, the AOC [23.15a]. Men feel abandonment by their money-whoring Mother, aka the USA Inc. Government.

I love my Gay friend even though I know it's been declared illegal in the Second **Cunt-Situation** [17].

Yep! In **Amendment** twenty-nine [17.29.1] it states Man-on-Man sex (gay) is illegal unless it happens for training purposes.

Pssss… How did we go down this path son? Where did the USA Inc. go wrong? I mean, why I should have to fill-out a training form after I suck a dick! Sperm protein should be a nutritional supplement!

I totally agree with you Sir. And the **MOM69** [4.D-G5.6] form is a bitch to fill-out. Hey! Dr. Yanket, we're not trying to cause problems for any group in our society. I mean, in my scheme we'll just be targeting American men, who by no fault of their own had their penises shrunk by our government.

Right Son, during the, Great American Penis Shrinkage Phenomena, the **GAPSP** [23.17]. And Seymour, I had nothing to do with the shrinkage!

Yes Sir I know, that whole USA Inc. government program was way before our time. Shrinkage went into effect after the, National Emergencies Act, the **NEA** [25.12.1], enacted on September 14, 2176.

Well, anyway **Seymour**, no offense intended to our Gay friends, but I don't even think there're that many gay men in the non-interned US population.

Sir, you mean because most of the gays were designated as domestic terrorists and put into FEMA detention camps?

Yeah **Seymour**, they were made to bend over and provide "special" services to the FEMA guards and government officials. So where we gonna get all these Homo… Whoops! Sorry, I meant gay men?

Well **Sir**, let me explain, (Seymour back peddles realizing he is only an assistant researcher and is putting his neck out on the line with his scheme), the resource is hidden!

Seymour, do you mean all the Gays are in the closet?

No! No, no… You're thinking of crossdressing bisexuals. The resource is in the shadows.

Do tell, do tell young man… (Dr. Yanket says to **Seymour** with a skeptical frown in a disapproving tone).

Sir! It's all about size. It's the size that counts not the queerness!

Ahhhhh… And son, you're not gay right?

No **Sir**! But I kinda go both ways, if you know what I mean?

Well **Seymour** I'm fine with your orientation. And from

speaking to you I can tell you're a fairly intelligent young man. Still, I think we got side-tracked here. Just back-up and explain what the hell you talking about?

Thank you **Sir**. Their penis size Dr. Yanket, not the gayness of the man-cunts is what matters in my Sex-for-Labor scheme.

Huh! Haaaa haa… Okay. Please tell me more about this wild outlandish fantasy **Seymour**. Wait! You sure you're not gay?

No **Sir**! But my cousin Sam in Cincinnati is a flaming queer and he has a really small, peanut size dick.

Haa haaaa… Thanks for sharing **Seymour** but spare me the details about your family members and please continue.

Right **Sir**, well if you think about it, the gay cum-munity is one of the last resources we haven't exploited in the USA Inc. But it's not the solution. Although we might be able to utilize the gays for training purposes!

Okay **Seymour**, I'm concerned for you, are you on medication?

Ahhh… Well yes **Sir**, of course I am. Nowadays all American's are required to be on some kind of mind-control meds, the **MCD** [6.F.3] issued by the DHMC.

Oh, yeah, yeah, the US **Surgeon General** [4.D-G6.11] has written a refill-indefinitely, open prescription for antidepressants for all USA Inc. citizens. Well **Seymour** anyway, I don't count mind-control as a medication. There're considered a life-style supplement. (As Dr. Yanket pops a handful of who-knows-what pills into his mouth).

Right Dr. **Yanket**, I've been on opioids since I was an infant so they just create a state of mind. What really affected my life were the things which happened to me. They made me who I am. For example, when I was small a psychiatrist dry-humped me which aroused me then I creamed in my pants. And there was a time in the military where in the shower I dropped the soap and the time the priest fuc….

Whoa! Okay, okay. Geeez! **Seymour**, skip some of the juicy parts and please continue.

Right, so anyway, this is the way I see it working Dr. **Yanket**. We can start a program where we employ males with extremely small tiny penises and I'm talking small, two or three inches max. Researchers call them, micropenis, but on the street they're called, Cockettes, cocklets or boy-clits, pencil-dicks.

You're sounding more gay by second here **Seymour**.

Well Dr. **Yanket** it's sad but at least 69 percent of men in America nowadays who because of their poor quality of life have had their dicks shrunk.

Right **Seymour**, like we were saying during the, Great American penis shrinkage phenomena, the **GAPSP** [23.17].

Yes **Sir**, after the Economic Holocaust of 2007-2008, the government encouraged American men to be less aggressive physically and emotionally. This caused a lot of erectile dysfunction.

Right, right. **Seymour**, which then caused the US government to commit Economic Sodomy on American men. It's the leading cause of males losing their manhood in this Cunt-trie. Especially Bankers, Politicians, Cunt-gressmen, Lobbyists and Corporates. It's a shame these dudes ended up having a much smaller penis length compared to the rest of the males in the World.

Sir, on this point let me remark, these men have no jobs, no money, purpose-in-life and consequently no females in their lives. The male population in the USA Inc. is just be cuming a dickless depressed group.

Right, right **Seymour**. Huh! I heard they think the government is like their mother. And they're trying to suck on the mommy money-tit.

Well hey Dr. **Yanket**, whatever, but these men could be exploited by us because they have a serious problem attracting the female members of society to engage in sex with them.

Right, due to their pinky size dicks?

Yes **Sir**, like for example my effeminate cousin Sam.

Seymour, I get it! This is all sounding plausible because like you were saying, considering nearly the entire female population here in the USA Inc. is practicing abstinence from sex.

Ahhhh… **Sir**, mainly due to there being no contraception drugs available in stores or clinics anymore.

Seymour this is true. Besides, the grim fact, the conceived child would possibly starve in a FEMA camp, is another grim reason not to knock-up a woman here in the States.

Correct Dr. **Yanket**. It's really sad our Cunt-trie became this dispirited and downhearted about their future.

Yes **Seymour**, these are very dark times for the USA Inc. Okay so let me get this straight, the lack of sex partners has only increases male horniness to an epic proportion? Which reduces their desire to work? And their penis size is controlled by the government?

Yes! Yes! And Yes! **Sir**, they just hang-out at FEMA camps and play with themselves.

Hmmm… Well **Seymour** I see your point, what are we going to do with these less endowed pansy fellows?

Sir! Sir! Remember, tone down the slurs and slang about Gay people? Let's just practice a more respectful vocabulary, please?

Whoops! Sorry **Son**, yeah, yeah. I'll tone it down. Okay, if the non-gay, heterosexual American male worker doesn't want to poke a guy in the ass?

Dr. **Yanket** the way I see it, the lowly, extremely lonely, small-dick male population, which in actuality, is probably no more than a bunch of, drugged-up, cross-dressing, heterosexual drag-queen, fake Sissy, closet feminine, jerking-off, pseudo faggot, wanna-be queers who need our guidance!

Wow! Tsss… **Seymour**, you're holding nothing back there. Huh! Haaa haa… Ahhh… Your scheme is sick! Very freaken sick!

Yes, but obvious Dr. **Yanket** they're sexually useless and also wife-less members of society, which could and should be fully exploited.

Wow! Exploitation? Huh! It is an American attribute if you think about it. Imperialism, Interventionism.

Yes **Sir**! It's as if our USA Inc. government shrunk their Willies so we can go ahead and exploit the American male population. It's like a new form of White-Nationalists, Penis-Nationalism. Where the size of a penis rules.

Now you're talking my game **Seymour**. I mean, you seen my dick, I'm hung like horse. Shrinking Willies, hey! More pussy for us right? The more dickless men there are in America, the more cunts available.

Huh! **Sir** you're sounding a little misogynistic. Pssss… But yeah, I guess you can say that, regardless of dick-size. I'm sorry exploited is such a harsh word. I meant to say, we need to encourage these men to participate in a new profitable industry called, Sissy Sex Labor Compensation or something!

Okay this still sounds really, really queer, gay, whatever appropriate way you wanna call it. And leave my gay-friends out of this!

Oh! Right! **Sir**, they have nothing to do with this scheme we're plotting. We'll only exploit who our government created through penis shrinkage.

But hey! I'm all out of ideas about how to improve the economy. So please go on **Seymour**. Tell me more my new friend and colleague.

Well **Sir**, my plan is way more complicated than some fancy **Hardon-Vard** [3.C1.10] university economic theory. You see, at first we could start a program which would provide as much **sex** as the American male working population wants by using these adult Sissy guys. The Sissies would be providing sex for the hard working men who have a regular, productive, government provided, full-time job. The workforce would boom in size!

Hmmmm… Yeah… Sex… (Dr. Yanket has got his hand down his pants rubbing his dick). Hmmmm…

We would have all the happy, ball-drained, morally bankrupt, hardworking men we want by providing them free holes to bang. And seeing how men are so horny due to the female abstinence from sex, they'll screw anything! I heard men are doing it with, cows, chickens, goats, monkeys, dogs anything they can stick their dicks into!

Yes, **Seymour** I get your point son. The situation of abstinence from sex is horrible out there, and those freaken government issued **Chastity-Belts** [7.G1.11] are a bitch to get off! But what would make the working male population suddenly gay enough to stick their dicks into these Sissy boys you're talking about?

Ahhh... They're horny?

Yeah of course they are! And hey! I've poke a Ladyboy or two in the ass on my trips through the sex capitals of the world and mind you it was just safe recreational sex conducted for research purposes only.

Hmmm... Ahhh... Sure it was Dr. **Yanket**. As interesting as your card games with your gay-friends, I imagine?

Right, right **Son**, you know what I'm talking about, wink, wink, (The good doctor winks at Seymour who by now fully understands Yanket's sexcapades with trannies and also his cherished relationships with his gay-friends). Just a little poke in the hay, some fun on Uncle Sam's dime. Ummm...

Yep! Been there done that Dr. Yanket. Those Trannys Gurls are really hot. Hmmmm... (They're both getting kinda cummy and start openly stroking their crotches). Ahhhh....

Son! I like you. We're grown men, adults (Dr. Yanket whips out his huge dick again and starts stroking it in front of Seymour). Go ahead son, you can whip it out, we're not gay! This is the new heterosexual way! Anyway, we can just fill-out a **MOM69** form if caught doing naughty stuff. Here's a form,

```
┌─────────────────────────────────────────────────────┐
│                                                     │
│  MOM69: Man-on-Man Sex-Training Requisition Form    │
│                                                     │
│  Dominant Participants (M1) Name: _____   │
│                                                     │
│  Subjugated Participants (M2) Name: _____   │
│                                                     │
│  M1 Penis Length: _____                   │
│                                                     │
│  M2 Penis Length: _____                   │
│                                                     │
└─────────────────────────────────────────────────────┘
```

Well yeah! What the hell. Why not! Ahhh… (Seymour, although a little embarrassed, follows suite and exposes his not so big manhood to his boss). Yeah, I go both ways **Sir.** Like I said but not if the other dude isn't receptive.

Well, to each his own, my friend. **Seymour** look, if you're that insecure about Man-on-Man play, just stay over there across the room and we won't have any problems. Huh! But your feelings are pretty obvious to me. I know your uncomfortable with it, but your Gayness is showing. I mean, you haven't stopped staring at my big beautiful dick. Ahhhh…. All this Gay talk has got me turn-on! Ahhh… Ahhh…

Geeezzz… Me too. I'm ready pop, **Sir**! Ahhh…

Here, here. Ahhh… For instructional purposes, let's watch this Hentai porn on the flat-screen! Yeah **Seymour** you're kinda small Son. You been drinking the government Cool-Aid? That shhh…it will shrink your pecker!

No! No! I only drink filtered water. And **Boss**, I'm small in the manhood department from birth, I was born small. But I love wacking-off to crossdressing, trap Hentai cartoons! Ahhhh… Thanks for putting it on.

Sure, sure… Here **Seymour**, I bet I can hit the waste-basket from all the way over here! Ahhh… Ahhh… Try it son! But I warning you, I can shoot pretty far! Back in high school I always won the ejaculation contests! Ahhh… Ahhh…

Ahhh…. Well, I'm so small the coach wouldn't let me compete, so my personal best was only six inches. Ahhh… (They're both wacking off as fast as they can). Ahhhh…

Haa ha… Wow, pretty short son, **Seymour** I hold the record at my college fraternity at nine feet! Ahhhh…

Moments later, Yanket shames his assistant…

Wow! Perfect shot! Great frapping off **Son**. Sorry the basket was out of your range for you.

Well **Sir**, you're obviously a better shot than me. You made a direct hit in the basket. Congrats! Good shooting Dr. Yanket (Seymour was just put to shame yet compliments his boss in a congratulatory tone).

Practice **Son**, practice, it takes practice. But hey! Son (Yanket says in a parental voice while patting his assistant on the back), I wouldn't get your hopes up too high with a prick as small as yours. Okay! What were we talking?

Ahhh… I think we were discussing men banging Gurly-Boys? Something about how homophobia may be an issue.

Yeah, yeah… We were talking about a large change here **Seymour**. The way I see it son, most American men would be reluctant to buy into your wild scheme.

Agreed! **Boss**, let's face it the majority of American men are macho, heterosexual homophobes!

Exactly! They screw girl cunts. So what makes you think they're suddenly going to start mounting guys and screwing them in the ass? I mean no matter how horny they're! I just don't see your scheme happening **Seymour**.

Booty… Booty… Booty… Booty… (The booty-call ringtone sound of Dr. Yanket's secretary messaging him). Okay! Lunchtime! Gotta go! (Yanket jumps out of his office chair with anxious anticipation).

Whoa! Time and Jizz sure flies around here, (Seymour checks his watch). You're right **Boss**, its lunchtime!

Yeah **Seymour**, I always treat my secretary to lunch.

Wow! You're very generous, **Sir**.

Well, not exactly **Seymour** you see, my balls are bursting. This means I need to relieve myself by feed her a liquid Jizzzie protein snack for lunch.

Oh! Like you do with your gay-friends **Sir**?

Yeah, yeah, of course I swallow, who doesn't nowadays. But you didn't hear that from me **Son.** Here, open-wide! Only effeminate boys with little dicks like you admit to swallowing. (Yanket jokingly elbows Seymour in the rips then scoops up a wad of Jizz from the waste basket and sticks it in his new scheming friend's mouth).

Ow! Guk! Ooouuugh! Gross! Okay, I know nothing! (Seymour chokes on the sperm wad). I see nothing, I taste nothing!

Exactly! Good boy! So **Seymour**, let's pick-up this conversation after a break, I'll be fascinated to hear how you solve homophobia in the USA Inc.

[1.5] GENETICS

After lunch they reconvene…

Ahhh… I feel so much better after emptying my balls. I got a great Secretary. **Nora**, that little whore, is my favorite.

Yes **Sir**. Nora is pretty hot flaunting those 48DD tits of hers. I mean, she wears see through blouses, so she's obviously putting her jugs on display.

Huh! **Seymour**, well cum to politics! I'm the director of health and mind control, the **DHMC** [4.D-G6.1] for a reason. The Cunt-gress knows I supply free pussy with my office staff. So, how are we gonna do this sex-labor scheme of yours. And if it works, our scheme (Yanket mooching in on the credit).

Dr. **Yanket**, it cums down to supply and demand sex-economics. I took a course in college on sex for money. The only thing I remember about it was the term project was orgasmic.

Right, right, sex-economics, fun term projects, I re-took that course six times, or was it nine. And your sex for labor scheme could work but, we cum up short on the supply side. Where are all these fuckholes gonna cum from **Seymour**?

Well Sir, it's a wild concept and you're right, we can't pull this off with just a bunch of Sissy-Boys. Like I was saying my plan is huge. The fags…

Whoa! Whoa! **Seymour** I thought you said we weren't gonna be socially incorrect with our terminology?

Yeah, sorry about that, **Sir**. We need to watch-out what we say. Okay, maybe we can just call them something more gender neutral like, Cock-Lovers?

Yeah, yeah, yeah **Seymour**, why not. It sounds better than just saying Fag! It still sounds like an innuendo but at least we ain't insulting anyone directly. Cock-Lover, could be a cross gender, gender neutral slur, right?

Yeah, yeah... Let's go with that **Sir**. So, Dr. **Yanket** we can have a **Phase I**, to just get the whole program started. Then with some genetic engineering voodoo we implement phase II.

Very interesting, go on **Seymour** I'm with you.

This is my main idea. I know this research scientist in the USA Inc. working on a human genetic engineering project. I discovered her by accident when I was working for **DARPA** [25.26.1].

Oh! The Deep Advanced Raw (un-protected) Penetration Agency, DARPA? Isn't that where they do all the freaky Frankenstein stuff?

Yeah DARPA, they conduct all kinds of shady experiments. She uses the detainees from FEMA detention camps just like the US government does for most of its dangerous biological freak experiments. And she's made some huge breakthroughs in gene manipulation.

Wait a minute, so how did you accidentally run into this scientist?

Oh, well I wasn't being paid much, so when I saw a notice on the office bulletin board about a clinical trial. It pays the participants for having sex with a new experimental animal. And I'm like, hey free sex! Why not, right! So I signed up.

Wow! **Seymour** you're like stud man!

Well not exactly. But in the end, I never got a chance to poke the creature, it turned out my dick was considered too small for the trial. It was kind of a bummer for me. I started getting all conscience about my size and withdrew into depression over it.

Ah too bad **Seymour**! Cheer up son (Yanket has his arm around his assistant to console him). Besides, it cums down to performance not size.

How so Dr. **Yanket**? I mean, I grew-up being told size matters.

Well **Son**, it just impresses the ladies if you have a long pole, but under the covers in bed it really cums down to how you can wear her cunt out.

Wow! Huh! Really? I was told just the opposite of that! (Seymour is in total disbelief). Haa haaa…. Dr. **Yanket** you're just saying that to make me feel better about my pecker size.

No **Son**, I'm serious, it doesn't matter how long your dick is, it matters how long you last in the bitch! Believe me. I've bang many women in my life, it cums down to how long you last and how many orgasms the girl has.

Wow! **Sir**, you're saying all these years I had it all wrong about women.

Yep! **Seymour**, it all changed for me when I started reading about the **Casanova** [25.28] techniques the Latin lovers use. That's when I became the Love-Stud I am today. You just gotta bang them mercilessly till they beg you to pop your load. Tssss… By then, they've had so many orgasms they would say anything but still you get what I mean? Get them to beg for it!

Casanova, hmmm… Yeah Dr. Yanket, I'll read up on it. But anyway. Like I was saying, learning about what was going on in the laboratory was more valuable than getting my dick wet.

How so? It sounded like a freak show, sex with animals?

Yeah that's what I thought at first. But who gives a shhh….it! I thought I discovered the answer to our economic failure! Think about it, a new genome called the Homo-Sis-Sapien. Pssss… moral convictions was the last thing on my mind.

Wait, wait, Sis What?

Homo-Sis-Sapien genome explained…

Sis as in Sissy. It's a cross-genome animal! This hot scientist chick figured out how to get the male body to have female features. Like the elimination of facial and body hair, increased hip width, all the feminine features of the female body, also the creation of breasts, voice tone, and penis size reduction. The whole transgender thing in a test-tube.

That's crazy, but exciting! (Yanket is recalling having sex with shemales and rubs his crotch). Ahhhh….

Yeah! And she's thought of everything, the gene modification drugs created in her laboratory can reduce the height of the Sissy so they won't tower over human men making the male feel inferior if the Sissy wears, whore type six inch high heel pumps or eight-inch platform shoes like the hookers used to wear.

Wow! **Seymour** is it real? You fantasizing?

No! I mean yeah **Boss**. Every little detail of their faggot, Whoops! Sorry, Cock-Loving bodies can be modified by the gene mutating drug to make the Gurls look like real human Girls.

Geeezzz… **Seymour** she's a genus! (Yanket has is hand down his pants again yanking on his fuck stick). Ahhh… tell me more son, where's the waste basket?

Yeah! She's an absolute genius! She produced two versions of Sissies in her DARPA test lab. There's a **D-Type** [1.1] formula which mutates the Sissy into having conservative domineering mannerisms, a huge three inch Gurly cocklet, tiny little balls, a small yet very attractive, female frame, of only five foot tall, huge lactating tits. This type is called the DOM for dominant. The D type was designed to maintain control and manage the submissive, subordinate, hyper-sexually aroused **B-Type** [1.A2.2].

Wow **Seymour**! There's a pair of them?

Yeah the B version formula, oh the B stands for **Bitch**, was created to be a Sissy bitch-in-heat. This version is much more sexually active than the "D" type and has submissive characteristics.

Ahhhh…. Ummm… I like what I'm hearing here Seymour!

Yes **Sir**, so the bitch-in-heat version is in a constant state of sexual arousal and will have sex with anyone. The Bitch type never grows taller than four feet high, and doesn't look a day older than seven years old over their entire lifetime.

Wow! Tell me more, **Son**! Ahhhh….

Oh and the really cool feature of the B-Type Sissy is, they produce more than three pints of jizz a day.

Whoa! That's a lot Jizz. Seymour, look at my balls, I don't even produce that much (Yanket, has his pants down while jacking away at his bone getting more interested in the new sex-toy his assistant is tell him about).

They're incontrollable cum spewing Hoes, **Sir**. I mean orgasms can happen at any time for no apparent reason. The B-Type [1.A2.2] is just a sex toy and the D-Type is the B-Type's master.

It's incredible **Seymour**! Son, can you take over stoking my manhood here, I want wolf-down this **Mystery-Meat** [4.D-G1.21] sandwich one of my wives made for me.

Ahhh… Yeah… Ahhh… Okay. Glad to be of assistance Sir. (Seymour reluctantly takes hold of Yanket's huge erect cock and strokes it while continuing his explanation).

Thanks, Chomp, chomp… Wow, this mystery shhh….it is disgusting! Chomp, chomp, chomp… Anyway, you were saying something about types of these animals, toys…

Yeah! The scientist who made the discovery, her name is **Jamie Goodass** [18.0.1]. She spent many years observing the behavior and getting shagged by the **Bonobo** monkeys [18.3].

Wow, you're saying, they banged her in the jungle? Awesome!

Yeah, yeah and one day when her cunt was sore she decided to return to America to work in the DARPA lab to create a bonobo pet to play with.

So **Seymour**, I guess the Military at DARPA wanted to weaponize it? I mean, even if it wasn't made into a weapon a hot monkey bitch like that could be used for recreational purposes for the soldiers.

Right Dr. **Yanket** and regardless of her motive. She figured out how to splice female vagina from the Bonobo monkeys in Africa who resolve their conflicts by having sex with each other, with the butthole of a flaming American queer human faggot!

Son! I thought we agreed to no inflammatory remarks? This office could be bugged, there might be someone listening to us.

Whoops! Sorry Sir, I meant to say, effeminate American men or Cock-Lovers or whatever. And Sir, I think you meant defamatory?

Yeah, yeah, thanks son, inflammation is a condition I get on my dick after I do all my wives in one go. And hey! I'm no literary master. Erotica novelist can spell better than me!

Glad I can help, **Sir**. All we have to do is not say anything derogatory and offensive. Okay, I gotta switch hands. My wrist is getting sore stroking you.

Sure switch! Well let's back-up here **Seymour**! Anyway even if we name them appropriately, you pretty much lost me. You mean a Monkey and Fag combination? Haaaa…haa… So how does any of this make sense? Because, they're two different genomes!

Yeah, yeah, she calls this all-inclusive ass-crack a, **Vaganus** [14.O1.6]. It's a vagina-anus combination without an active uterus.

Wow! Hard to believe! Freaky but awesome. You mean to say it's a hole which is both an ass and a pussy, an ass-pussy hole! Hmmm? Un-fucking-believable! Seymour, I'd throw you out of my office if you weren't such a good cock-stroker. Ahhhh…. Yeah, yeah, like that. Keep stroking me. Ummmm…

Doctor **Yanket** it's my pleasure to be of assistance to you and your needs. (Seymour is really trying to score points and takes the bold initiative to kisses the tip of Yanket's dick to show respect for a superior). Kisss…

HEY…!!!... Whoa! What are doing?

Sorry **Sir**! (Seymour gets startled by the Yanket nearly jumping out of his chair). Just wanted to show some respect, Sir.

Seymour, (Yanket says in a firm voice). Just keep stroking my shaft. You're doing a fine job. But don't do any of that Gay shhh…it on me. Heck! We're two grown adult men here. I mean, for Jizz-Us sake! We're colleagues, if you want me to stroke you, as you stroke me, I'm fine with that. Ahhhh… Okay, now tell me more about what a Vaganus is, Son.

Well **Boss**, the Vaganus is like the Holy-Grail of sex!

Hmmmm… Yeah… Stroke it son, this Vaganus thing is turning me on. Hmmm…. Yeah, that's it, stoke the whole length. Yeah, like that. Ahhh…

And **Boss**, the most amazing thing is the mutation drugs even prevent birth defects from cross-breeding through incestual sex. So, we could have the genetically mutated humanoid Sissies fucking each other.

Wow! You mean in this new genome, daddies screwing daughters, sons humping mommies, sons mounting sisters and just popping out new faggots by the dozens like rabbits?

Yep! **Boss**, they're not humans, so they can screw whoever they want, Like in the wild.

Oh, my god! This is a total reversal of morality! Wow, it's sick, it's perverted, but damn! It might work. **Seymour**, I still don't see what it has to do with getting rid of homophobia?

Well, Dr. **Yanket**, we could make contraception illegal even if they could afford to buy it on the black market. Also continue to prohibit pre-marital sex with the mandatory government issued **Chastity-Belts** [7.G1.11]. This way we force the horny male workers into having sex with the human girl-looking mutations and eliminate the homophobia via their shear desperation for sex.

That's one problem. What about the cunt volume needed?

Well **Boss**, like I said we need to start with **Phase I**. Before we can breed enough of the almost perfectly modified, close-enough to real female mutated Sissies, we need to get the program started with human Sissies.

Okay **Seymour**, so Phase I will be human fags. Whoops! I can't get the F word out of my mind. Can I say queer?

No, no, no, not that either! None of those insulting words or phrases. Only correct appropriate terms. Remember Sir, most American men had their penis shrunk during the Great American penis shrinkage, the **GAPS** [23.17]. Many men are still sensitive about the loss of masculinity.

Got it! Thanks, I'm not trying to be insensitive or anything. **Son**, keep stroking please. And do continue. Ahhhh….

Right in **Phase I**, the program would take advantage of the government created emasculated population. We'll inoculate the existing, useless, small-prick, adult American males with the Sissification drug.

Right, right, round-up the non-wealthy, small dicks.

Exactly, then we can start a test program where we feminize the crap out of the little-dicks. We'll get them literally into action, screwing, looking and acting like real Gurl-Cunts.

Okay, I'm with you **Seymour**. Then what?

Then Phase (II) is started when we have enough breed from birth non-human genetically mutated Sissy livestock. Until then we fake the workers into thinking they're really screwing a girl-bitch right.

Okay, but they're really banging a queer up-the-ass?

Yeah, yeah, Dr. **Yanket**, something like that. I mean at first, sure we, stick a bag over the heads of the not breed from birth adult Sissies. And have those non-queer heterosexual hard working men mounting the somewhat sissified ladyboy in a dark-room.

Right, right, right, dark room, bag over the head…. Sounds like a card party I attend occasionally. Ahhh… You're actually a better stroker than my secretary **Seymour**. Ahhhh…..

Sir, after the initial introduction period needed for the Sissification drugs to really take effect, our horny American male population will be banging away at those feminized, Gurly looking, dress-wearing, Sissy-Boys with reckless abandonment!

Haaaa haaa ha… Yeah, this is the exact description of the wild card party I go to. **Seymour**, but will they figure-out what kind of hole they're in?

Hell, Dr. **Yanket**! They won't be able to tell what hole they have their dick in or what gender for that matter. As far as super horny men are concerned, they could be doing a goat, I mean, a hole is a hole when you're horny! Right Sir?

Sure, sure I get it **Seymour**. I mean personally I have six wives to take care of my sexual needs. But as far as the working population is concerned, we'll have the large workforce we need to build the new stuff by providing unlimited sex.

Right Doctor, we can build all of it. All the great scientific discoveries we seized in the Financial World War, the **FWW** [23.24].

But some folks say the New Industrial Revolution or the **NIR** (EN02) started because of all the stuff we stole in the war.

Right, right. But hey **Seymour**, nobody wanted the War. But the Eurasians were out thinking us! We only started it because the USA Inc. tried to shut-down the **WTO**. Our allies were pissed-off and joined together with the other nations to form the Eurasian Union. The US got screwed over. So we had to make a first strike.

Sure, Doctor **Yanket**, you don't have to justify the greed of the USA Inc. The main thing is, we'll be able to create the workers which will enable us to manufacture here in the US once again. No more of that Globalism bullshit!

Exactly **Seymour**. And the American male population will be in a delusional state of mind with unlimited hormonally raging sexual activity, sounds great! But wait! Like I was saying, do we have enough Gurly-Boys for Phase I? Ahhhh…..

Well, hang-on Sir.

Son, Ahhh… You better put your safety goggles on, I'm gonna blow a load soon. Ahhhh….

Yes **Sir**. Thanks for the warning.

And how many of these mutated Sissy boys can we create and how fast? Do we grow them in test tubes in a lab or something?

Whoa! Slow down Dr. **Yanket**. Ah, I'm not a scientist but mathematically, if you figure three or four penetrations per week per male workmen and a workforce of two hundred million horny American males. Hmmm (Seymour scratches his head with one hand while stroking the boss with the other) and at the rate of two hundred dicks a day per Sissy with a five day work week. With one thousand penetrations in the ass-pussy.

Ass, I thought you said it was a modified vagina?

I'm sorry Boss, in the **Vaganus** per week per Sissy. This means we would need roughly eight hundred thousand or more Sissies.

Holy shhh…it **Seymour**! It's nearly an inventory of a million of them! It would take forever to produce this many chicks with dicks!

You're right Dr. **Yanket**. In Phase I, its gender reassignment not queer creation we're dealing with here. We're just giving this profitable opportunity to these men with pathetically small peckers. Being gay or turning queer is just an option or a side-effect not a requirement. It would take a program spanning decades to develop a sufficient amount of trained Gurl-Cunts.

Jizz-Us!

Yes, like I was saying in **Phase II**, I suggest we breed the Sissies from birth. We'll use financially desperate parents as volunteers from FEMA zones as hosts to grow the mutant non-human Sissies. The Sissies will actually be nothing more than cash collecting sex machines with personalities.

Grow the Sissies?

Yes **Sir**, one little Sissy boy-bitch at a time.

You're nuts Seymour! (Dr. Yanket slams his fist down on his desk).

Yeah, I know Dr. **Yanket** but it's all about providing the utopian world of an unlimited sexually active and productive, hardworking society. And thanks to the world changing discoveries, we immediately need all the labor we can get.

I agree, the discoveries made by the scientists and engineers the USA Inc. has acquired or captured in its imperialistic conquest of our Allied Nations. Allies which were dependent on the Federal Reserve issued US dollar. And let's face it. These US Allied Nations were merely puppets of the United States.

Yes **Sir**, I agree with you. And using sex as labor compensation is just a new way to control the American worker from a different angle. I mean, we'll never get to Mars and declare it part of the new American Empire if we don't start producing more stuff.

Right! And rebuilding the huge military-industrial complex our great nation once had before the US Petro-Dollar collapse.

Yes **Sir**. And the key here is the Sissy boy-bitch. We'll need lots and lots of them!

Hmmm.... **Seymour**, pay workers with sex! Hmmm.... It's a long shot. Boy is it a long shot. But damn it might just have a chance. Hell, it's our only chance. Maybe we can call the process, the Labor Compensation Transaction, the **LCT** [4.D-G2.27].

Sure we can call it whatever we like, it's never been done before!

Look **Seymour**, I'll propose this mutant Sissy thing to compensate workers to the administration and see what happens. From what you've told me the technology is there to produce these genetically modified, mutant livestock animals as whores! But the timing is an issue.

Right Dr. **Yanket**, we'll need to work fast to generate a feminine looking Sissy population capable of screwing millions of horny American male workers.

But Seymour for **Phase I**, where're we gonna round up all these interim adult males with small dicks to get the program started prior to growing-out the mutant Sissies from birth?

Well like I said, in the short-term, given the desperation of the USA Inc. population due to the lack of employment, food, water, toilet paper, sanitation, free-porn, condoms and other essentials like soft-drinks, we could launch a massive propaganda campaign.

Sure we'll us the Hollywood Propaganda Corporation, the **HPC** [21.B.17]. It could be something along the lines of, the US government is offering cash to patriotic men volunteering for the Sissification program.

Ah huh... haaa haa... And Doctor as usual the USA Inc. government, given its mastery of deception, doesn't have to tell the poor idiots what they're signing-up for. In reality they're going to be rimmed-in-the-ass. But screw-um, just promise them a goodtime and food. Hell most American's will work for food nowadays.

Hell **Seymour** for that matter, we don't have to tell them they're going to be Sissified either, we can call it procreative reclassification.

Yeah! Well shoot! 69 percent of Americans are so poor they're stupid enough not to know what the government's doing to them anymore! It's 911 all over again!

Brilliant Dr. **Yanket**. Sure and pump them up with Sissification drugs stick a dress on them and Walla! Then at the same time start a nation-wide research project to document the penis sizes of the entire US male population.

Right **Seymour**! We'll just tell the gullible American public it's for the war on **Terrorgasm** [4.D-G7.12]. Yeah the sheepeople still believe false-flag propaganda bull-shit.

Yeah like the 911 buildings magically falling down into their own footprint defying all the physical laws of nature. Weapons of mass destruction, America is a democracy and this is a good one, the War on Terror.

Exactly! Noble Peace Prize winners like **OBomb** have the right to kill people with drones! I tell yah American's are so gullible, Gulf of Tonkin, Pearl Harbor, 911. All either a scary fictitious concoctions and or sinister plot created by our banker controlled black-ops shadow government agencies instilling fear in cowardly gutless Americans.

You got that right Doctor **Yanket**. They've been lied to so much they're delusional. Americans don't know *what-the-fuck* is going on. Sir, do you want me to continue to yank on you?

Yeah, keep stroking it son, you're doing a job. Right, Americans believe in mythological fairy tales, not reality! Ahhhh….

Oh yeah! With the HPC propaganda machine cranked-up we can make them shit-their-pants with terrorism fear crap. It's right out of the Fascist playbook.

Oh! I know **Seymour**. We can tell them a scientific study by Hardon-Vard University [21.C.12] sponsored by the New World Order Organization and the **UN** [25.8] proved only virile, large penis, hormonal raging, males are strong enough to fight the domestic terrorists.

Right! You mean Terrorgasm.

Yeah! And all the small dicks, three inches or less, need to register for the Sissification program.

Huh! And regardless of how your dick got that small. Even if it shrunk by drinking the cool-aid the USA Inc. government gave you or not.

Yes of course so they can support our brave troops who are going *door-to-door* defending our Nation, flushing out the evil terrorists who are being harbored by traitors here in the United States Incorporated!

Hoe! A perfect pile of horse-shit if I ever heard one.

Right, right, they are sheep. They'll believe whatever we tell them.

Oh and it should be considered the patriotic duty of every American male with a less-endowed penis to join-up to be sissified and help his or her or whatever you call Sissies, Cunttries fight against the evil enemy bad guys!

Bad guys?

Does it matter? Whoever the hell they may be! Pick one! Which to our demise is everyone not cooperating with the United States Incorporated?

Yeah! The enemy is at the gates! We'll work them up into a nationalistic frenzy. Be a real American, stick a girly dress on and bend over for your country! Haaaa... haaa... haa...

Right, right... Haaa haaaa... Kind of like a *Rosy-the-Riveter*. Except instead of women working in factories like they did during World War II, they'll be USA Inc. civil servant Sissies working in Whore-Houses!

Perfect Dr. **Yanket**! But it would need to include participants of all age's especially young boys. Boss, do you want me to stick a sock on your dick Sir? It's gonna pop a here any second Sir.

Ahhhh…. Nah! Open-wide and swallow **Seymour**! Ahhhh…. Yeah…. Down-the-hatch Son. Good Boy! Get used to swallowing. (Seymour reluctantly swallows the load to save from being fired, knowing all alone that gay sex is an illegal act).

[1.6] MORAL ISSUES

Wait, wait, wait a minute **Seymour**! What did you say before I popped my load? Here's a napkin Son, you have Jizzzies on your face. You need to look professional around here.

Thanks for the napkin, **Sir**. I was saying, we need young boys too because… (Seymour says cautiously, but gets interrupted quickly by Yanket).

Whoa! NOT KIDS! NO-FUCK-WAY! We'll be breaking all the **Sex-Laws** [7] based on stopping pedophilia. (Actually at this point in the development of the new economic system, the MSES, they haven't yet created a sex-law to legalize having sex with the Sissy animals).

Yes, but like we said **Sir**, these are hard times, our fiat currency is worthless and the workforce participation problem needs to be remedied now if the USA Inc. is going to dominate the world again through Democratic-Imperialism.

Damn! So what are you suggesting **Seymour** and this better be good, Son?

Well Dr. Yanket, one thing we can do is, change the child molesting laws in the United States to make it legal to have sex with and only with the officially registered test-tube created humanoid, trained Sissy Whoring animal.

I do like it! It's wrong **Son**.

Sir, the child molestation laws for regular human kids, the non-mutant, non-Sissy normal kids, would still be enforced. We're still morally correct according to the Cockolic Church cum-mandments.

Ohhh… Ohhh… Okay, okay… Whoa! You were scaring me there **Seymour**. Wooo… Though you were crazy for a second there! We wanna stay morally correct.

Yes, yes… I understand. The **Homo-Sis-Sapien** [18.3], the Sissies, would be registered in the US Federal Governments Sissification® Breeding Program as, not-from-earth, aliens. And they'll also be certified by the US Department of Agriculture as livestock animals.

Okay! So the Sissies are animals not human?

Yes **Sir**! This way the registered mutated non-human young animals, or kids as we call our human youngsters, are the only ones who can legally have sex with the working adult male population in the US.

Okay, okay… I'm with you. Okay Seymour, and considering the mutated Sissy is not actually a full-human being, the pedophilia laws shouldn't even apply to them.

Yes this is correct Doctor **Yanket**. Besides, we work for the USA Inc. government, which means we can do whatever and fuck-whoever we want.

Exactly! Fuck-the-laws! With the passing of the **PATRIOT** [23.22] Act we can screw whoever we want. I mean, not fully-human is technically like saying the genetically mutated Sissy is just an animal, like a chicken or a goat or a sloth or, well you get the idea right? I mean a cop isn't going to arrest a guy for porking an under-aged cow in the ass or for that matter, an older one with sagging utters, Ugh sick! Haaa... Haaa....

Haa... haaa ha.... (They're both having a chuckle over sex with animals). Okay, I follow you on this Dr. **Yanket**. I'm not sure sloth would be my first choice to describe our patriotic overzealous nationalistic, bend-over and take one for the team, mutant Sissy friends.

Right and besides, us Neoliberals are in control now! All the, left-wing, socialists have been eliminated or put in a FEMA camp or beaten into submission by the state controlled media. Free speech, transportation, rights to bear arms, property ownership and other frivolous freedoms are all under federal control now. We won't hear much out of the child-abuse assholes.

And if we do **Seymour**, they'll be dealt with by enforcing the US Patriot Act and **NDAA** [23.21.a] like our government does with everyone else! Control is the key here in the land of the free Aristocrat and home of the brave Capitalist.

Sure **Sir**, I mean screw Cunt-gress and the new Cunt-Stitution we'll just get an executive order signed by the President. Besides the opposition would be considered terrorists if they try to stop us from supplying non-human little girly-boys to be freaken banged in the ass by hard working productive Americans.

Ummm Hmmm... Who's going to care if a little Sissy boy takes it up the ass regardless of the age of these puny pinky sized dick

Gurls anyway?

Right! And like you said **Sir**, I'm not sure if we could even consider them to be human despite their human appearance. Actually after we genetically modify them, they'll just be government owned and operated livestock animals utilized for labor compensation through sex.

Hmm.... Sex with almost human young boys, still sounds absolutely illegal but, interesting at the same time.

Well **Sir**, sure and it would still be illegal if the child is not officially registered as a Sissy by a veterinarian.

Of course **Son**, we don't want anything to happen to our future, hard-working strong American Stud children, now would we?

No **Sir**! God forbid anything happens to our future workforce.

Right, right, the wealthy float to the top to managerial positions and the small dicks fall to the bottom of the manpower barrel?

Exactly! And beyond this Dr. **Yanket**, we can implement laws to prevent abusive treatment of these young underage hyper-sexual Sissy creatures when engaged in sex training.

Underage, now that's a dirty word **Seymour**.

Sure it is Dr. **Yanket**, but the young Sissies, regardless of them being from a different genome, won't be able to perform fully as Whores till they are physically and mentally trained to be so. Think about it, an entire segment of the American male population either being breed, transformed or trained into being, sucking, fucking, walking, talking, like women, dick-loving professional Whores. They're just a bunch of sex-toys for the workers to abuse. It's an Unfucking believable concept!

I agree **Seymour**.

Great Dr. **Yanket**! Because you realize it's all well and good for the Sissy freaks we breed out of test-tubes but the human Sissies recruits would have to be mostly young boys?

Wait! Again! Not human kids? Like I said NO KIDS! Why kids **Seymour**? Where you going with this?

Well, older men in dresses, think about it?

Ooooh, yeah, I see your point, definitely a scary picture.

Yes Sir, super scary! But hey! Granted for the adult human Sissies with the right amount of Sissification drug therapy, make-up and queer training provided by the gay cum-munity, the older adult Sissy recruits will be cum more and more lady-like over time.

Hmmmm... Chicks with dicks, (Dr. Yanket pulls his limp cock out again) interesting! Ahhh….

Yeah **Sir**, you keep thinking about boy-pussy. Because we'll have to utilize the young human Sissies kids too....

NO! NO WAY **Seymour**. I said NO! It's just wrong! I mean don't you think we need to feel sorry for these human Sissies kids? Geeez! They're just kids!

Hey Dr. **Yanket**, these kids don't really have a choice now do they? Their tiny little pinky size dicks are big girly clits not manly cocks. They don't have a place in America's future because it's a pretentious male dominated world. So we'll be doing them a favor by putting them to work in Whore-Houses.

Well look **Seymour**. I don't give a

Shhh….it…!!!...

About the adult faggots but the human kids I don't buy into this at all. We're not touching the kids! It's just wrong!

I'm sorry Dr. **Yanket**, you're absolutely right. I forgot to mention, our scientists have all of this worked out.

Geeez! More science? Okay but I'm telling you now **Seymour**, I don't care how much Science crap you got, NO KIDS!

Okay this is part of **Phase I**. You see they do this thing called Transmutation, or **TM®** [2.B2.11]. It's done to the young under-aged human Sissy recruits.

Sounds weird! I don't like it.

It is **Sir**. Transmutation is where their genome is changed from Homo-Sapien to Homo-Sis-Sapien. It's simple. The Sissy candidates all need to be in prepubescent early childhood and not older than eight years of age for the transmutation to work biologically.

Wow **Seymour**! Does it actually work? Changing genomes, this is wild! It's Wee-Ooo-Wee-Ooo, tin-foil hat shhh…it!

Oh yeah Dr. **Yanket**, it sounds like science fiction all right! And for the most part, 69 percent of the time the **transmutation** process doesn't work and the results are horrific. I mean they survive the failed process nobody ever dies from it. But they're grotesque creatures if they do. Physical deformities like, they be cum feminine, grow big tits, nice ass and have enormously large pennies.

Wow, it sounds like the Gurls down on K-Street where the

lobbyists hang-out. Ahhh…. Tits and ass, I'm all ears!

Yeah! Chicks with Dicks your favorite **Sir**! However the rejects as appalling as they may be, get tossed back into whorehouses in the FEMA camps where all the recruits came from.

Hmmm… Whorehouse, so what's the problem? What were they doing in the FEMA camp?

Well **Sir** honestly, in the FEMA camps most of these kids are sexually abused young children, they're forced into being whores. They would have died at an early age anyway from starvation, blood borne pathogens or sexually transmitted deceases.

Huh! That's horrible **Seymour**!

Yeah, if they don't die from deceases they get abandoned and tossed into a dumpster. So if the **transmutation** process works we're doing them a favor by giving them a new chance to live a longer healthier life.

God **Seymour**! It sounds awful! Gruesome boy body parts changed into Gurly parts. Abandoned children! What have we be cum in this Cunt-trie?

Sir, I agree, it sucks to be an American. But we're covering are asses, we get signed permission forms from their parents if they have any, right after we liberate them. The parent's permission relieves the government from any liability.

So **Seymour** we're basically in the business of rescuing abandoned children?

Right **Sir**, the problem is there's a very small window of opportunity for those who qualify for the non-breed-from-birth

Sissy classification. The lucky kids we recruit all get **transmuted** from human to humanoid.

And if they're older?

The over eighteen small pecker adults, well, we've discussed this. Nobody really gives a shit about them! So there's no need to feel guilty because there'll never be humans under the age of eighteen who work as Whores performing labor compensation.

Oh okay. Wooo, I was worried there for a moment.

And Dr. **Yanket** besides if the adult Sissies start whining like little Gurly-Boys we'll just play the nationalism card and tell them it's their duty as an American to be patriotic and bend over. But we might experience another problem with recruited Sissies if they have an inferiority complex about their small penis size.

How so **Seymour**?

Well, if their dicks are not long enough, say for example, like my own penis, (Seymour fishes in his pants for his tiny pecker and lets it peer out at his boss).

Wow, you're small **Son**.

Yeah Boss, nothing to brag about I agree. So if men with my condition are homophobic about being recruited into the Sissification Program we could have riots on our hands. And end up with a displaced portion of society with bigger than girl clits and smaller than well-endowed stud penises!

You're right Seymour. We'd have to construct an entirely new society with this **Sissification** Breeding Program (SBP). We would have to re-classify the entire US population into specific social classes and sub-classes also specify the benefits for each.

Yeah, yeah… I can see that, **Sir**. Maybe, Gurly-Whore, wealthy Stud-Elite, and the smaller than dicks but bigger than clit types, the lower in cum, they can be called, Non-Stud worker-laborer minion class or something... Yada, yada, ya…

Yeah! Whatever **Son**. Well talking about classification.

Boss, I think I'm just a little below average at four inches when erect. So I won't have to worry too much about getting recruited as a Sissy, but you on the other hand. Dr. **Yanket** your thingy is obviously a Stud-Cock.

Oh, yeah, you've stroked it **Son**. (Yanket has his dick out and is stroking in front at Seymour while giving his assistant a knowing glance). It's above average if six is average. I'm about fourteen inches erect I guess. Go ahead Son, I know you wanna stroke it again. Ahhh…

Wow! Hung like a horse dude! (Seymour grabs his boss by his Cock and starts stroking its length). Ahhh… You like that **Boss**?

Yeah, yeah **Seymour,** stroke my Cock like all my other colleagues do, from the President on down. I'm proud of it. And my six wives suck and slurp on it every night like it's a candy cane. They all love the damn thing!

Yeah I see why. You obviously have a real Alpha-Male, Power-Cock **Sir**.

Well, let's not worry about the homophobes, sizes and Studs just yet **Seymour**. What we need is legislative changes in Washingcum on Capitol-Hill. Ahhh… Faster Son. Ahhh… Stroke it! I gotta a feeling you're gonna be cum my new Boy-Bitch! Ahhhh… Yeah…

Sure Doctor **Yanket**. And yeah, we need to infiltrate the Law-

Makers for results like the Lobbyists.

Yes **Seymour**, Ahhh… I'm going to talk with some Cunt-gressional cronies about this and hopefully we can get our corporate contributors to pay enough of them off and get this program started right away.

Awesome Dr. **Yanket**, I'll be with you every step and stroke of the way! I'll be at your side the whole way, Sir.

Good! Ahhh… This is huge **Seymour**.

You are **Sir**. It has to be the biggest Cock I've ever saw!

True! But **Son**, I'm talking about our plan to save our Cunt-trie. I mean we might be looking at having to write several new amendments to the **Cunt-Stitution** [17].

Yeah, yeah, or possibly a whole new social class system all together! **Sir**, this reminds me. I got a strange message the other day from this Chinese-American Chick, **Sue Yan Nish** [21.20].

Chinese? Shhhh…. Keep it down **Seymour**. There're a few things you never say out loud around here in Washingcum.

What's that **Sir**?

Chinese and Fag, never say either of those two words around bureaucrats. They all know, fag's and the Chinese are really smart and super-clever.

Well you might wanna make an exception **Sir**. She said it was a research paper about a Social Class solution for the New America. I opened the attachment and was amazed at how detailed it was. Maybe we can implement it in our new system? She calls it the **MSES** [23.13].

Yeah sure, **Seymour**! Let use all the free shhh…it we can find. The Chinese are brilliant at social order and harmony. But **Son**, we'll have other problems. We might have to get rid of a couple of moral convictions.

Sir, this could be a new world when we're done with it.

Yep **Seymour**. Ahhh…. Stroke me Boy. Ahhh… And a bunch of morally conscious Senators and a religious cum-mandment or two or three. Ahhh…

Dr. **Yanket** this is a, make it or break it moment in the history of the United States Incorporated. And it's a perfect time for a dramatic change. We'll be draining swamp!

Well, it's beyond a drain job. We'll have to douche it out!

Right but **Seymour**, I can use a good ball draining. I'm almost there Son. Ahhhh…. Yeah… I'll do the paperwork, go ahead Son, get on your knees, you're gonna have to take me orally. Ahhh… I'll have to get all the credit of course, but I won't throw you under-the-bus Son. We'll make a handsome profit from the scam, I mean scheme.

Guk, Gak, Gck… (Yanket tries to shove his massive Cock down Seymour's throat). Slurp… Wow, you're very big **Sir**. Do your best to get our plan to work. Gek, Guk…

Well our Fascist President, money whoring law makers, corrupted paid-off Supreme Court judges, Lobbyists, Federal Reserve cartel bankers and the international corporate thugs who destroyed this Cunt-trie, are either under investigation, standing trial, imprisoned, murdered or executed. Ahhh… Almost!

Glrglk… (Seymour pulls it out to respond). So Sir you're saying this could be a fresh new start for a once powerful and great nation? Guk, Gak…

Slap! My Plan. It's my plan **Son**. Keep suck Bitch! (Yanket slaps Seymour wanting to instill a fear in him).

Yes Sir. You can dominate me, I'm fine with that. Kisss (Seymour kisses Yanket's cock head to prove his loyalty to his Boss).

Ahhh… Right Seymour! Obey your Master! Slap! Regardless of how immoral it might seem to build an entirely new social class who takes it *up-the-ass* for the sake of its Cunt-trie. Let's just fix this hollowed out **Empty Nation** of ours while we still have a chance! Now! Now! Oooooh! Fuuuuuck! Swallow it! Ahhhh….

Guk… Guk… Guk… Gulp (Seymour reluctantly swallows down the whole wad of his chauvinistic boss in hopes that he doesn't lose his job over his submissiveness). Glrglk… Glrglk… (Choking sounds). Ouuuugh! (Seymour throws-up some of the massive wad of Jizzz). Thank you for the protein snack **Sir**.

Well **Seymour**, well cum to the new America! And I like you. I'm glad you understand your position and swallow like a good-boy. My advice, if you wanna keep your job, is to get used to it.

Yes **Sir**. (Seymour says while shamefully wiping the Jizzies off his mouth). I will obey.

Yes you will **Son**. And as my new Executive Assistant I'm gonna make you my Boy-Bitch®. Just follow my orders regardless of the humiliation it might cause you.

Thank you for the opportunity **Sir**. And good luck with getting the approval from the Cunt-gress, Dr. **Yanket**.

Chapter: 2 Program

[2.1] MSES COMMENCEMENT

Ten years later….the year is 2232...

Wild ideas indeed! But we put together a program which is designed to, pacify, cultivate and mind control the entire male population of our country. Gentlemen sex is a powerful tool which has been used throughout the ages to manipulate others. Here in the United States Inc. sex for the first time in the history of the world will ingeniously be utilized in a payment system for labor.

Yay! Yah! Clap, Clap, Clap… (Applause).

And I have had the honor and privilege of working side-by-side with the brilliant man who is the architect of the most ambitious social and economic program ever created, I now give you the Director of the Department of Health and Mind Control, **Dr. Hank Yanket**.

Yay! Applause... Yay! Applause.... Yay! Applause....

Thank you **Seymour**, thank you everyone for your applause, thank you, thank you. I'm happy to announce to all of you finally after an initial testing period, the Sissification Program, the SP [4.D-G2.2] is ready to go into action nationwide through the joint effort of the, US Treasury Department, the Department of Labor, as well as some other, not to be mentioned, government pseudo politically controlled agencies and orgasmizations.

The Modern Socio-Economic System (MSES) is a complex system created not only to support the Sissified® Cum-munities throughout our Nation, but also as a structure for everyone to thrive economically and socially with equality for all who we deem worthy of such privileges.

Clap, Clap... Yay! (Applause from some). We need jobs man! (The crowd is heckling). Free drugs! Got no Money! We ain't got shhh...it! (The dissidents are dragged out of the audience and thrown in a van to be hauled away to a re-education facility in a FEMA camp).

It wasn't easy! We had to craft a new **Cunt-Stitution** [17], the Second Constitution of the United States. But the alternatives where dreadful, if the MSES was not implemented, if science did not prevail with gene manipulation, if we didn't take advantage of one of our last resources left in our great Nation, the penis-size challenged male population of this country, than our Nation would have fallen back into total collapse.

Yay! Yay! Applause.... We love you Hank! (All of Yanket's six wives and nine housekeepers are jumping up-n-down with their huge boobs flapping for him). Yay! Yay!

And thanks to the contributions from our government officials, scientists, gay-folks, military, religious, pharmaceutical industry, medical cum-munity and corporate benefactor's prosperity once more is becoming a reality. This reality is, our workforce being miraculously resurrected out of the caldron of poverty. A workforce not based solely on education or skills but on its horniness and a hope for a new life of testicle draining sex and an everlasting supply of Sissies. Applause, applause, applause....

Thanks for your applause, thank you, thank you, thanks again and God Bless American Sissies.

Well, Seymour, (Dr. Yanket and Seymour shake hands) we did it!

Hey, we got a lot of work ahead of us Dr. Yanket, I have to give an opening speech in an hour at a Whoring Station on K Street, in Washingcum DC, wish me luck.

Sure good luck, screw a lobbyist for me!

Ha haa, very funny. Lobbying is illegal now.

Yeah maybe they all turned patriotic and became Sissies this is where all the new money is nowadays.

[2.2] WS369C

Whoring Station, WS369C...

Thanks for your applause and for inviting me to the opening of the new Whoring Station **WS**® [7] number 369C. I'm proud the Sissification Program (**SP**) is getting off the ground in your cum-munity. There's been a lot of support for SP here in the Washingcum DC area. As you will certainly find out, the Sissification Program is emotionally and financially beneficial to your whole cum-munity. And it's a benefit not only for those precious biologically modified creatures we call Sissies. It also includes the human host families and every citizen depending on their penis size.

Clap, clap, clap... Yah! (Applause from a crowd pumped up on the government issued antidepressant drug MCD).

Thank you. And I know what some of you are concerned about when you think about Sissies living in your cum-munity. Things like safety. Notions such as, are our children safe around the mutant **Sissy**® creatures. All I can tell you is, a Sissy has never failed a US Department of Agriculture Vaganus® probing inspection. So we can safely assume they are completely disease free! Also Sissies have never been found entirely guilty of violating any of the, **Three Laws of Sissies** [15]. You can find the Laws in the WS369C brochures and in the Sissy manual SM069.

Section 15, Appendix P, SCWE, the Three Laws of Sissies

So, you and your families are perfectly safe. Believe me the Sissies are very docile creatures. Like most animals, their more afraid of you then you are of them.

Applause.... applause.... applause.... Free Pussy man!

Thank you... thanks for your applause. Getting back to the benefits of having Sissies in your cum-munity. It's important to realize the registered Sissy-Breeding program families receive a large animal breeding compensation payment per year per Sissy. And the benefit is spent back into your cum-munity. Also the salaries of the many trained professionals make up the large dedicated group of Sissification Program (SP) specialists are employed and profit by keeping the SP running smoothly.

These Sissification Program Specialists make up the growing Sissy Support Service Industry which is approximately 69 percent of the American labor force now. To name just a few of the careers and businesses in this booming industry we have, the Sissy Sexual Trainers (SST) who are the Sissy families Live-In Sissy Trainer (LIST). The Sissy equipment manufacturers who produce fantastic products like the, AutoSuck®, AutoPenetration®, Douche-a-Matic®, PrettyPuss® tester and the Labor Compensation Bench, the **LCB**® [22.4], products which are installed in all of our Whoring Stations WS®, Whore Houses WH®, Cum-munity Sex Recreation Centers and Special

Integration School System, **SISS** [11]. The SissySeat® installed in all Integration Schools. And to promote equality amongst Sissies, the SissySeat® is equipped with size adjustable probing wands. This accommodates the appropriate vaganus penetration depth depending on the particular Sissies capability in different age groups.

Oh! Let's not forget the medical professionals, the proud nurses and doctors who probe and perform medical procedures. Like the Compensation Orifice Widening Procedures, **COWP** [4.D-G1.2] and Pussy Blooming Procedure (PBP) preformed on Sissy-Gurls® who are ready to take the promiscuous step into becoming a Sissy-Lady® by having a permanent prolapsed Rosebud.

Also there's the Penis Official Length Certificate, the **POLC** [4.D-G1.3] and the Cum-O-Holic Rehabilitation Centers (CRC). All of these are vital to the health and wellbeing of our most precious resource, our proud American Sissy Patriots.

Applause… Applause…. Go Sissies! Applause, Clap, Clap…

And of course the invaluable contribution of the accountants and computer programming nerds who handle the Sissy Sexual Activity Auto-Accounting System, **SSAAAS** [4.D-G1.26]. The signal transmitting antennas are embedded inside each Sissy hole. And also around all the penises of workmen, which keeps an accurate account of who and how many times a Sissies hole has been penetrated for the good of all of us.

Applause…. Whooohooo… Yah Sissies! Yah! Free Pussy!

Thank you, again thanks for your applause, your support and cooperation with the SP in your cum-munity. Thanks and happy ejaculations to all of you hard working Americans.

Oh! And just a reminder. I see there are a lot of youngsters in the crowd today. To use the WS® facilities you must be eighteen year or older. Thank you!

[2.3] FIRST TIME

Seymour inspects the WS facility…

Mr. Goldberg! Now for the demonstration (Seymour and the manager handshaking), I'm Matt the manager of the Whoring Station 369C or just WS369C.

Please call me Seymour.

Well Seymour do you want to get started?

Yes, very much so Matt.

Ok, well Seymour I have a special treat waiting for you at labor compensation bench 69 or just LCB69. I chose this Hoe for you because I trained this Sissy® myself.

Right, all the Whoring Station managers have a Sissy Training Certificate, an **STC** [4.D-G4.3] and are Category one, Stud-Class [1.A1.1].

Right Seymour, WS® managers all have foot-longs. I have a Cock Ranking Privileges, a **CRP** of L12 [5.E2.1].

Okay! Here we are LCB69. This little Whore assisting is just a Junior Sissy Whore, a **JSW** [2.B2.2] so she's just gonna do the fluffing today.

Fluffing? (Seymour questions Matt).

Yes, this JSW will expertly suck on your dick till it be cums

typically call them Sissy-Gurls® not boys. And never call a Sissy an (it). They're very sensitive creatures! Heck! They'll start crying if you call them an (it). But you know all this Seymour. It's all in the Sissy Manual, the SM069.

Sure Matt, but you know how the government works here in the USA Inc. My assistants, assistants, assistant wrote the manual, I have no-fucking idea what's in it!

Ironic! Huh! Okay anyway. Now these creatures have been Sissified, they're part of the feminine Sissy world. And despite having a tiny little penis they shed their association with the masculine in their new lives as proud American owned Sissies®.

Yep!

In fact, they have their own Worker Sub-Class in the MSES® called Sissy. And they're a Sub-Class of the Whore Class. So Sissies play an integral part of the whole grand scheme of social restructuring using the MSES model. Our Sissies here at WS369C are trained psychologically as well as physically to be Professional Whores and are classified by the Bureau of Sex Classification, the **BSC** [4.D-G6.4] as females not males.

Holy-Cow! Matt, all I know is whatever we call them, what a talented cocksucker this one is. I mean Wow!

Yeah Seymour, they have to get really good at it, really fast around here! I got thousands of hardons walking through those doors every day and these little Sissy holes have to handle every single one of them. Well it's a well-known fact Sissy gurls blow better than most human women in the Worker/Stud Class of society. Sissies win most of the National Fellatio League (**NFL**) Championships here in the United States Inc. [23.52]

But in reality it wouldn't be a simple comparison between

Worker Stud-Class women and Sissies. Because, as you know these Sissies are one of three types. (1) Destitute abandoned children who have been mercifully gene-modified by the transmutation process, a **TM** [2.B2.11]. (2) Adult humans who transitioned into Sissydom called Sissy in Training, a **SIT** [1.A2.4]. Or (3) Pure American Breed-from-Birth, **BfB** [2.B2.12] started in a test-tube and then a human female host carries the Homo-Sis-Sapien fetus to term. So the quality of their vaganus, the Sissy Ass-Pussy, varies significantly.

Well enough of all this Sissy-Science crap Matt, I'm blown literally away by this six year old mutant Sissy-Gurl®. Her ability to voraciously suck my dick is incredible.

Oh yeah! Well Lisa, the one you just got fluffed by is one of my favorite whores; she's a **B-Type**® Bitch Sissy [1.A2.2] and has milked my dick plenty of times during practice, all twelve inches of it. But she's too young of a Sissy to take it in her **Vaganus**® [14.O1.6] on a bench just yet. She can only be a fluffer and suck dick for the time being.

Well Matt, she is definitely eager to suck!

Oh yeah, She's a Breed-from-Birth Sissy, a BfB and they're usually the most sexually active Whores and much better than an assimilated non BfB, transmuted TM Sissy.

What's a BfB again?

All American quality Pure Breed-from-birth Sissy, they're **PBS** [2.B2.10], the best we got! I'm surprised you don't know this Seymour!

Hey Matt, all I know is she was hungry for dick!

Seymour, there's a reason she's hungry for your manhood. You realize Man-Cream® is the only food a Sissy consumes. And their sucking enthusiasm has a lot to do with their need to feed?

Yes, of course I know! I designed the Sissification Program this way to keep these tiny nymphos constantly hungry for men. I just never got to experience the trained finished product of our wild perversely concocted idea of a utopian society full of peace, love and constant Sissy-Sex®.

Ahhh… **Seymour**, I think the Manual refers to it as **Bonobo-Sex**® [22.19]. Didn't our government patent the process?

Whatever Matt. But six years old, wow! I didn't know we had to start them so young.

Yes, well, the rule in the manual states they have to be at least 13 years or older, enrolled in a Special Integration High School and have passed the, Associates Sissy Whore Exam the ASWE, to work part-time in a Whoring Station on a bench for training purposes only. In other words, according to the rules a Sissy can't be used for penetration till they pass their **ASWE** [4.D-G4.6].

Well then this little Whore is way too young to even be here, Matt!

Seymour! I couldn't agree more. But the new Executive Order, No. EO111169 from the President made it mandatory to have all the Whoring Stations open 24/7 and to reduce the waiting time needed to mount the whores down to just one hour or less. We had to drop the working age requirement down to accommodate the Presidential Executive order. We're just desperately short of trained Sissies Seymour! And we're especially short of the high quality Breed-from-Birth Sissies, the BfB kind.

Yeah but they're just kids Matt! Even though they're just

animals we might be crossing the line here.

What can I say Seymour? These young under-aged Sissy Whores are not even old enough to be Associate Sissy Whores (ASW). Hell! They haven't even finished their Sexual Integration elementary school education yet or taken the ASW exam! Seymour, they got me using JSWs instead of ASWs. The next thing you know, they'll be telling me to use, Training Sissy Whores, (TSW) on the benches. I tell you Seymour, this has got Sissy abuse written all over it! I get death threats all the time by Sissy civil rights activist groups, accusing me of animal rights violations.

I just don't know what to tell you Matt, but it's clearly stated in the twenty ninth amendment of the Second US **Cunt-Stitution** [17.29] that USA Inc. male citizens have the right to penetrate Sissies regardless of their age for labor compensation. I mean, we conduct financial transactions when we screw a Sissy. And we had to give the American workers something other than worthless dollars for their labor or they wouldn't work, it's the American way.

Dark-times Seymour.

Matt, don't get me wrong! If these little mutant freaks weren't animals created in test-tubes I wouldn't be screwing them at all, I'm not a pedophile!

I didn't say you were Seymour!

Matt, there're laws against screwing little human kids. And the ones violating the **Sex-Laws**© [7] are the dumbass, small dick, Non-Studs.

Right! Right, they're nothing more than a bunch of sick perverted assholes! They see no measurable difference between mutated humanoid Sissies and real human kids. I say send all the sex offending Non-Studs to a FEMA Transmutation Center, to a **FTC** [4.D-G6.8] and stick something up there ass just to see how much they like being abused.

Yep! Lock-up all the perverts!

Oh yeah Seymour, Geeez… Round-up all those perverts and stick them in a zoo! And we definitely have the rights provided to us as Americans by our second Cunt-Stitution. It would be un-patriotic not to screw a **Sissy**®. I mean the mutants are nothing like real humans. The Sissies have gonad glands which produce sixty to ninety times the amount of semen as humans do. So yeah, they're just cum-spewing freaks! Human looking monkeys!

Right Matt, when they're fully transmuted at a FTC, from human-to-humanoid **Homo-Sis-Sapiens** [18], Sissies only have about a 95 percent match with human DNA, more or less the amount a chimp has. So yes, the Sissy has a different genome than Humans yet are very similar. In many ways a perfect match to humans in respect to the way they look, walk and talk, but the real difference is the Human-Bonobo Sissies screw like animals!

Well Sissies are animals Seymour.

Yeah Matt. And hey, I know what you mean about Sissy abuse. I wrote a report to the, House Ways and Means Committee stating everything you just told me. I know they're too young to start a career in the Whoring industry.

Good! Somebodies gotta tell those folks in Washingcum what's going on in the Whorehouses!

Matt, my report made it clear, there has not been enough time allocated to breed and train the Sissy population prior to the launching of the MSES. But you know the prerogative here in

America; someone has to take it up the ass if we're going to make a profit, I'm sorry, I mean progress.

I agree with you Seymour and it was clear when you drafted the rules for the Sissification Program, there's a copy of the, Sissy **Classification** [2] Rubric posted in every Whoring Station.

SM069, Section 2 Appendix B, Sissy Whore Classification

Well anyway, we're going to make it as pleasant and as safe as possible for these precious little Sissy-Girl cum-moddities.

Matt, twenty years from now we'll have plenty of these little genetically modified mutant Sissy princesses to go around. Hell maybe we'll start exporting American Vaganus® to other countries.

Haaa haaaa... But for now we just have to satisfy every horny worker we can, anyway we can.

Huh! Good luck Matt, but I got to get this Whoring-Station visit over with and be on my way. So, where's the little mutant hole I'm gonna abuse?

[2.4] LCB

Okay, right here, LCB69, and here's your Whore, her name is Mandy, her number is 6989369, she's a JSW, just turned eleven years old and it's an illegal age to be penetrated in a public Whoring Station by any Stud or Non-Stud. Typically JSW Gurls can only engage in sex with, Sissy Family members, a Live-in Trainer **LIST**® [4.D-G3.2] or a Sissy Trainer Certified an **STC** [4.D-G4.3] Stud. This is all specified on the Sissy Whore Classification chart. And on top of that, she hasn't even had her Associate Sissy Whore Exam, her ASWE yet.

So Seymour, sorry if you were expecting a more mature and qualified Sissy Whore. I'm also disappointed we don't even have a **B-Type** [1.A2.2] or even a, Breed-from-Birth, a BfB for you. Mandy here is just a sissified boy.

And by this you mean she's been through an FTC a FEMA Transmutation Center [4.D-G6.8] and is a TM® Sissy?

Right! So in reality she's not her original human self anymore after transmutation.

But hey, never mind all the government rules and genetic crap. The real issue is she's too young, under-trained and over-fucked.

Yeah Seymour, you can put it that way. Hell! Like I said, she's not even old enough to legally mount a LCB® at a Whoring Station facility yet. She's supposed to be home training at her families Whore House with STC Studs and family members.

Unfucking-believable! It makes me wonder what Frankenstein world we created at the Department of Health and Mind Control?

Seymour, I seriously don't know, but the USA Inc. economy needed something to jump-start it.

I'd don't know Matt. This is looking more like a mistake the more I see how it's unfolding into just another government control trap. (Seymour is starting to have doubts about the whole MSES scheme).

Hey Seymour, cheer-up buddy! Just look at that juicy piece-of-ass on the bench waiting for you to mount her!

Uoooh! Yeah, she does look delectable! The way she's spreading her pussy lips for me. Ummmm… Nice! Very, very nice! (Like turning off a light, Seymour just totally forgot about the inhuman economic scheme the Shithole Cunt-trie he works for has planned for its destitute population).

Hey! By the way, if you want to check her Whoring stats, there's a mini-tablet which all Sissy Whores at a Whoring-Station must have available. You can see, (The manager browses the tablet for the Whores info).

Cool, everything is so modern here in the WS. I wish the rest of the Cunt-trie wasn't in such disrepair.

Yeah Seymour, the USA Inc. might be a shithole but at least we have the best Whores! Here, Mandy was discharge from the FTC and certified a TM® Sissy on 06-09-2229. Her serial number is, TM02472869NBFB. She only has three years of Whore training. She's a transmuted (**TM**), a non-BfB and her pussy has only been widened by the COWP twice so far. So judging by your width she might be a little tight for you Seymour.

But none the less, Mandy's Sexual Skill Rating, her (SSR) is impressive at 8, and her Sexual Activity Rank, her **SAR** [5] is high for a Sissy her age. She's achieved the rank of, **Daisy** which means she's had, 20,000, Sissy-Pussy penetrations. If you ever want to check the Whores Sexual Activity Rank, the SAR chart is posted at every LCB® in the Whoring Station.

SM069, Section 5, Sexual Activity Rank (SAR), Appendix E

She's only a **TM**® but I'm still proud of her, like I am about all the young Sissy Whores who work here. Mandy is going to be a hot little Professional Sissy Whore someday. She can easily handle a man like a Professional.

Tsss… **Matt**, where do we find all of this raw American talent? It's amazing!

Good question **Seymour**. Like I was telling you, most of them are abandoned children. America has been through some hard financial times. Most everybody is out of work, 69 percent of folks don't have jobs.

Or they stop looking for one. Hard, hard times for the non-wealthy. Good times for only the Lobbyists, Fascists and the rest of the Autocracy in the USA Inc. So where did we cum up with all these potential Whores?

Well, for example, Mandy here, we found her raped and starving in the trash. It's where we find most of the Non-BfB little faggot boys we transmute into meaningful members of society.

Whoa! Hey, ease up on the defamatory remarks Matt. I still have a lot of friends in the secret LGBT cum-munity. It's bad enough they were forced into going under-ground or had to go on the down-low to make themselves appear like heterosexuals after the Second Cunt-stitution took effect.

Oh sorry man! I didn't mean I don't like Gay folks. And hey Seymour if you ever wanna do a Man-on-Man thing, my supervisor is an extremely wealthy High-Ranking bureaucrat who always approves the **MOM69** [4.D-G5.6] forms I submit.

And just between us guys, I spend most of my days bending over for or giving blow-jobs to my Boss. So I'm kinda into the whole, Male Anal Hole thing, the **MAH** [5.E5.10]. (Matt winks at Seymour).

Huh! Good to know dude! Same here. I'm only an Assistant Director, so I have a dick in my mouth most of my time at work. (Seymour winks back at Matt with a naughty smile). Anyway! So you find these displaced kids?

Yeah, yeah and fact is, if we didn't pull Mandy here out of the trash she would have starved to death in the FEMA camp. This makes transmutation even more relevant to the welfare of America.

Huh! Yeah Matt, I guess living is better than dying.

Well I mean, their human parents or the USA Inc. government obviously didn't give a crap about these frail little creatures, so why should we?

Wow! Talk about dark. (Seymour is just shaking his head about the way this Stud dude who was just cuming on to him switches direction and casually talks like life didn't even matter).

Anyway! Mandy's special, she was selected for the Sissification Program based not only on her miniature size penis and femininity. Also because she's from a large family who practiced incestual-sex and ran an illegal whorehouse out of their home. Her flaming-queer, Sissy ass-pussy has been plowed since she was an infant.

Okay, so you're telling me she grew-up with a dick up her Boy-Pussy? Hmmmm…

Yeah Seymour! Let's face it. If not by the Bankers and other dregs of society, our government is gonna fuck us in the ass eventually! And from what I've been told, her diet consisted of only Man-Cream®.

Well **Matt** (At this point in the conversation, Seymour wants to make a path to the door). I guess experience counts even if the family was breaking the child abuse, incest and prostitution laws prior to when the Sissification Program was implemented?

Well **Seymour** before the MSES, the economy forced a lot of American families to run whorehouses out of their homes. I mean, these kids we find abandoned in a dumpster are just products of our abusive government here in the United States. We take these poor young little kids out of the gutter, and through the transmutation process turn them into respectable professional Whores, living descent lives as normal humanoid TM® Sissy beings.

I agree it's a shame **Matt**, all those poor human children forced into being sex-slaves. I'm just glad we don't abuse children any more in this Cunt-tree.

Definitely **Seymour**, we don't abuse human kids anymore in the

USA Inc. since we ousted the Fascists and setup the MSES. And out of mercy all the penalties are considered void for families who Sissified and became a registered Sissy Family of the Whore Class in the MSES. And like I said experience counts, especially for the Sissies who are older and non-BfB because the transmutation process doesn't wipe their previous memories. So once a hoe, always a hoe.

Okay, with all this talking it looks like you need a little more fluffing down there Seymour. Lisa Honey, help Mr. Goldberg get hard and ready to pop again.

Oooooh! Yeah, she's good! Oooooh! Good Gurl®!

Yeah, Lisa, suck on Seymour's dick like you suck on mine. Get him nice and hard sweetheart, give our guest a nice raging hardon ready to pop a load!

God Matt, checkout Mandy's smooth puckering little bottom hole as she lays there belly down on her LCB® with her ass propped up in the air waiting for and inviting me to mount her, she's so sweet! Oooh! She looks hot and ready! This is going to be like doing virgin pussy.

Seymour, Sissy Vaganus® is as close to a real human female's pussy as it can get. Plus these Sissy-Girls love to take hard dick up their lovehole! Sissy Bitch® types live to please men! They were engineered this way.

Yep! I'm so fucking-ready! Ahhh… She's a temptress!

Seymour, the seduction is all in your mind. Mandy's not supposed to engage in any kind of titillation with the men at a Whoring Station.

Right, right. This rule's in the Sissy Manual, under Sissy

Behavior, Section 15, sub-section 15-69, on proper Sissy sex ethics. [15-69.0].

Yep! **Titillation** performed by Sissies to sexually arouse men is forbidden by law and this goes for all Sissies regardless of their age, type, rating, rank or classification. And in this case I think it's your horniness Seymour, not a deliberate seduction by the Whore on the bench. We watch these little Sissy Gurls® very closely for lewd behavior. They're supposed to be acting like professional Whores not just some slutty street-walking prostitute.

Well anyway, you're hard again obviously, I'll just leave you to cream-fill this Sissy Whore and we'll talk later.

Okay Matt! Aaah!

Yeah Seymour, just let your fluffing Whore, (The fluffer guides Seymour into the Whores dripping wet cunt). That's it, guide it... Okay! There you go! Now shove your hard dick deep into Mandys sweet little bottom-hole.

Ahhh… Yeah! (Seymour follows the instructions and rams it all the way up the Gurls gapping wide lovehole).

Ok, there you go! It's in, perfect! See you in a few minutes Seymour?

Thanks Matt! (Sissy penetration achieved and the labor compensation begins).

Aaaaaagh! Agh! Ooooh! Yeah! Aaagh! Nice hole Mandy Girl!

Thank you Sir! Oh and I'm a Gurl not Girl. Slap, thump, slap (Mandy bucks back towards Seymour with every thrust he makes).

Ummm! Wow! Take it Bitch! Aaaaagh! I'm Cumming! Aaagh! I'm Cumming! Yeah! It feels so good to empty my balls! Aaagh! Slap, (Seymour slaps the young little Sissy on her ass), nice ass Mandy. Mwah...

Thank you Sir. I'm glad to please you. Mwah...

Thank you, Mwah... Ooooh, you sweet piece-of-ass. (Seymour pulls his soft dick out of her), good Sissy-Gurl! Mwah...

Moments later...

So, Seymour after emptying your nut-sack in that hot little Sissy, what did you think about the WS369C experience?

Awesome Matt! It was the best sex I ever had. And considering this is only a **C-Type** Whoring Station, I'm very impressed. As a married man who gets plenty of real vagina-cunt at home, I can see why eight-out-of-ten hard working American men prefer Sissy Vaganus® to that of a human vagina. Wow! This little transmuted TM® Sissy Whore sure knows how to please a man. I'll be back for more of her ass! Oh Dude, Mandy the little nympho, even jumped off her LCB, got down on her knees and sucked my dirty prick clean!

Yeah Seymour, Mandy's hot and she's only a Transmute, a **Mutt**®.

Right Matt, but her being a Transmute, this is more of a biological classification. Capability wise, I think it's the ranking. The SSR and **SAR**® [5] are what really count in determining if a Sissy is a good screw or not.

Seymour you have a point there. It's not like they need a Sissyology degree to be a good at emptying a man's nut-sack.

Well Seymour, it was a pleasure to have an official from the SP here. Thanks for cumming to the grand opening.

Haaa... haaa... haa, sure, sure, no problem.

And Seymour you'll always get full service here at WS369C. They get a lot of Sissy training and sex technique schooling here in the art of, man-pleasing. And not just a Vocational Sex-Ed education. [11] Whorehouses are a fully accredited part of the Sissy-Stud Integration School System.

Huh! Right, after all, these little Sissy Whores are the backbone of our Cunt-tries workforce now in the USA.

Yep! And even though, Whoring Station WS369C is only a type C our Whores put-out comparable to the kind of high quality sex you get from a classy, CSW or Branded Pimped Whores in an L-Type WS [7.G4].

Oh yeah Matt! This was as good as one of those fancy L-Type Whorehouses were they only let in the wealthy, High-Ranking Stud-Class, government bureaucrats.

Huh! And to think, the Sissification Program funding made all of this possible Seymour. What most men don't understand is a lot of women don't know the art of sex. Here, we train the Sissies to be a man pleasing Whore. And this is why hard working men just keep cuming back for more sweet Sissy-Cunt®.

Yeah this is the idea Matt. Keep them hard working men cuming back for more to get them ad-Dick-ted.

Right, you mean after the Federal Reserve printed our money out of existence, the US fiat currency was worth less than nothing. Hell, Sissy-Puss® is the most valuable resource the USA Inc. has left.

Yep! If it wasn't for the invention of the Vaganus® there would be nothing backing up the value of the US dollar! Thank the Cock-God© for your empty balls.

Amen!

And don't forget the proud well-trained Sissies! Amen again!

Well Seymour we're open 24/7 and like I said, if you ever want more quality Sissy-Puss cum on by and I'll make sure you won't have to wait in line to pop one out.

Sure will Matt! And thanks for an unforgettable experience. I'd love to stay and have second rounds on some of this choice Sissy you have here but I got a meeting back at the Capitol building with the Senate sub-sub-cum-mittee on Sissy Breeding Qualifications.

Ok, well good luck Seymour. Oh hey! Remember my offer about the Man-on-Man, the **MOM** [4.D-G5.6] thing we talked about. (Matt winks and blows a kiss at Seymour).

Okay I'll see yah again Matt (Seymour is surprised again by the offer, even though he swings both ways, he still has a hard time when men cum on to him).

Several hours later…

[2.5] SBQMC

Sissy Breeding Qualifications & Management Cum-mittee…

Dear Cum-mittee **Chairperson** I understand, but if these folks do not have the proper documentation of their families cock-size history, they're cock-lineage, or better known as **Cockage®** [7.G5.4], it's a mute issue.

Oh! For Cock-Gods sakes Dr. **Yanket** (EN02), the woman testified under oath, her father tried to rape her and failed because his dick was so small, he couldn't get his little pecker up her bottom-hole! What more proof do you want?

Chairperson, I know you have a lot of responsibility being on the Sissy Breeding Qualifications and Management Cum-mittee, the (SBQMC). But the rules have to be strictly adhered to. For all we know, this woman what was her name, Yowanda, could have had male relatives in her family with foot-longs, how would this workout?

Ah… I'm not sure.

Yeah, me either, but I can see something like this happening. We give the approval to breed Sissies based on her hearsay testimony of penis sizes in her family. Then, Walla! This mutant Sissy is born and he, she whatever, just happens to be hung like a horse. All because Yowanda's third cousins, grandfather on her mother's side of the family is a porn star. Do you see what I'm getting at here? We need to dig deep into their cock size lineage or we'll have problems down the road with cute macho Sissy studs with foot-longs, I mean the thought is horrifying!

Well, you got a point there Dr. Yanket.

Yes! And besides it costs us way too much money to screw-up the process! We're spending millions on each Breed-from-Birth **BfB**® [2.B2.12], genetically modified, mutant Pure-Sissy®. I mean these little faggots are costing the USA Inc. government a fortune to breed into existence. And even though they're just livestock animals we can't just grow Sissies like goats or chickens.

Yes, I'm aware of the costs Dr. Yanket. All the Sissification® is pricy stuff.

Yes! For example, did you know, we have to supply the Sissification® drug and nutrient fortified freshly bottled **Man-Cream®** to all the Sissies and to the families breeding them? And where do you think all the **Jizzies®** we put in the bottles cums from?

Ahhh… Whorehouses? I really have no clue. (The Cum-mittee lady is kinda bored with Yanket pontificating).

No! It cums from Non-Stud worker class male detainees and Transmutation-Mutts in **FEMA** [4.D-G7.13] camps. And from the Sissy and Stud Sperm Management, the **SSSM** [4.D-G2.9]. So we have to have a multitude of these FEMA detainees hooked up to milking machines just to support the Sissies nutritionally.

Yanket! Don't get me started about Creampies in my bed!

I'm sorry Chairperson, how many pies you collect in your cooch isn't my concern. How about we focus on the Sissy Sex Trainers the **SST®** [4.D-G3.1], yeah, the sex trainers are college educated professional sex athletes with a degree in Sissyology. They all have foot-long dicks! And they're all breed and trained exclusively for the job of training Sissies on how to perform labor compensation sex!

Also despite all of our efforts we're still in short supply of **SST®**.

Well Yanket, how are we recruiting these Studs?

Chairperson, we're currently recruiting qualified Stud parents to breed trainers with foot-longs to be the next generation Sissy-Sex® Trainers. We supply the Penis Enlargement Drug, **PED** [4.D-G1.11] free-of-charge. These Stud boys will be educated in the art of training little underage animals so they grow-up and be cum productive little man-pleasing Whores. But like I was saying, it all costs money and a lot of it!

Ok Dr. Yanket, I get your point, we're spending a lot on sex training and breeding but we need to increase the **Sissy**® population as soon as we can. And I'm under a lot of pressure from the budget Cum-mittee of the US Department of Labor about increasing the workforce participation rate.

Yes, I understand.

Right! They told me if we don't increase the amount of Boy-Cunts...

I'm sorry Chairperson, you mean Sissies? Please refer to the product appropriately.

Yeah, yeah Sissies. We need more Whores at the Whoring-Stations® across the Cunt-tree or our workers won't have enough cute little Sissy asses to penetrate! And then our production levels, the Gross National Product, the GNP, will go down dramatically.

Yes, yes Ms. Chairperson, I agree. As the Director of the **Sissification** Program [4.D-G2.2] I get all those reports as well, but what do you suggest? We stick a dress on some old guy, grease his ass, bend him over and let the horny workers have at him?

No, no, no, not at all. God-of-Cocks! What a disgusting thought! What I'm suggesting is to breed as many of these Sissies as we can with the hope most of them turn out to be authentic tiny little pee-pee type man-pleasing Sissy boys, I mean **Gurls**®.

Pee pees? Very cute Ms. Chairperson Pee-pees?

Well that's what my grandson calls his dick!

Well this might be cute, but I'll correct your terminology here and this is available in appendix A, of the manual,

SM069, Social Class Qualifications in the MSES

I'll quote from the Official Sissydom Manual, SM069, which I'm sure you've read cover-to-cover. In the document entitled, Sissy Qualifications, Document number: SQ10069, of the United States Sissification Act which Cunt-gress passed on, 12-23-2213, it states, a United States Inc. Sissy citizens penis is categorized as follows,

Category 4: cockette, any male or Sissy penis greater than one and less than three inches in length and category 5: clit, any male or Sissy penis smaller than one or less inches. Both categories 4 and 5, Class: Whore, sub-Class: Sissy, where the categories 4 is typically a **D-Type** [1.A2.1] Sissy mutation and categories 5 is typically a **B-Type** [1.A2.2] Sissy.

Thank you Dr. Yanket.

Sure glad to help. Now, my suggestion is this, we strictly adhere to the breeding rules set forth in the, United States Sissification Act and disqualify any Sissy® applicants who do not have the correct, Penis Official Length Certificate, **POLC** [4.D-G1.3]. And it must be signed by a medical physician who is a licensed Sissy-Specialist® and the applicants **POLC** is one of the acceptable categories of either, (4) cockette or (5) clit.

Thank you Dr. Yanket, I see your point you so arduously stated, we'll only accept tiny dicks into the Sissification program. I get it, emphatically get it.

Well good! But I think it's obvious the Chairperson is missing the point here.

Tssss…. Really Yanket?

Yes! The purpose of having Sissies with small pricks is to fuel the economic recovery! This can be accomplished through Sissies having a greater degree of submissiveness, humility, servitude, hyper-sexuality and abusability. And they courageously do all this despite Sissy culture being a particular segment of our Pro-Stud society, which has a lower demeanor, no self-esteem to speak of and fewer opportunities available to them.

Wow! I didn't expect a bleeding heart testimony out of a macho Stud character like you Yanket.

Hey Chairperson, I feel for these creatures. And this is not austerity. Sissies want to be abused! They love being slapped around, and enslaved into being owned by a master, which in this case the master or you can say Pimp, is the United States Inc. Government.

Again, wow! Dr. Yanket, it sounds like you take Sissydom® very seriously.

True! True! I do have a soft-spot for these little man-pleasing Sex-Workers. What I'm trying to get at Ms. Chairperson is, if Sissies didn't have tiny penises they wouldn't be submissive enough to sexually serve the larger prick Worker-Class® members of our Stud dominated society. And this would cause the entire **MSES**® [4.D-G2.1] to collapse which would create a social and economic catastrophe.

Okay Dr. Yanket, I see your point, please continue.

Well Chairperson, this Sissy-World I'm speaking of is an American designed and bio-engineered micro-culture in our Stud society. They beg to service men. They love to be humiliated in a way which befits their station in life. Their genes were mutated, and then they were born and breed to be servants of the working class.

I agree, I agree, men work hard if you give them enough pussy.

Exactly! They take pride and joy in sucking a human man's penis and swallowing the ejaculation. They also like being pissed-on and having sex with men who have much larger and superior Alpha-Type sized penises. Sissies proudly do what their government scientifically designed them to do. What they were meant to do. Kiss, fondle and worship penis! Trying to make a Sissy out of a non-mutated man with a normally endowed penis size is just a silly waste of time and an abomination of what the MSES stands for!

Whoa, whoa… Cool it Yanket. Get off your pulpit and just tell the Cum-mittee the fact, thank you. (The Chairperson has to rein in Yanket from his evangelizing).

Huh! Sure Chairperson, Sorry about that. What I was trying to get at is, it's a matter of pride. The parents of the Sissies are carefully selected from American families who have a long heritage of being mostly queer effeminate folks with small penises. And because of the break-through in bio-science and Sissy-Technology® we now can flip the Sissies from one genome to another, from Homo-Sapien to **Homo-Sis-Sapien** [18.3]. Same culture but transformed into a different genome.

Your point Doctor Yanket?

The Sissy livestock animals we're breeding in the **Sissification**® Program are not just genetically modified to be more feminine then the typical male. They're actually being raised to naturally be who they're supposed to be based on their family-heritage.

And in the post-dollar collapse era we're in, the Sissy culture is a large and expanding portion of American society. It's estimated to be approximately 31 percent of the remaining population here in the United States and the remaining 69 percent of males have been transformed into effeminate men. Hell, Sissydom® is an American phenomenon! Let's face it, the USA Inc. government committing **Economic Sodomy** on American men with the implementation of the **GAPS** [23.17].

Yes, yes, of course we shrunk the penises! So Yanket, what you're you trying to say? We need to embraces the Sissy culture! And seriously, only here in the United States has a government been this generous to give the registered Sissies their freedom and liberty to live dignified lives.

True Mrs. Chairperson.

And **Yanket**, this is regardless of them being classified as animals by the US Department of Agriculture. They only have a **Vaganus**® not a real vagina! But they're still raised from birth as Gurls®. They're trained to gladly accept men in all their holes without hesitation or regret.

Correct! They devote themselves as US Federal Civil Servant Whores to service the American male worker with their ass-pussies, which is sometimes confused as being a vagina. But their Lovehole® is actually a USA Inc. patented combination of an anus with a vagina called a **Vaganus**®.

Huh! (The Chairperson sighs). Thank you for that explicit description, Dr. Yanket.

Sure, also in our proud Cunt-tree, Sissies have the right to worship. There's even a religion for Sissies, it's called Cockolicism.

Right, right, the replacement one?

Yes Chairperson, actually it replaced the Catholic religion after the entire clergy was hanged for being pedophiles. The Holy Cockolic Church, the **HCC** [9] provides a spiritual haven to these Sissy animals. It teaches American Sissies to worship the human penis as their new god instead of the US dollar aka the old Federal Reserve Notes. They accept spiritually their fate as servants of working men here in the United States Inc.

Amen! And I'm pretty sure the Cockolic guys purchased the Catholic Church on the cheap after the pedophilia scandal.

Yes they did. But getting back to my point.

And Yanket, I'm still not sure what your point actually is yet!

Well allow me to finish. The Sissies who are raised from birth, the BfB [2.B2.12] in the Sissification® Program have no masculine feelings despite their DNA being predominantly male. They're raised as Gurls by inoculated human parents who treat them as feminine creatures. As I've mentioned, the Sissy animal is feed penis from infancy as their only food source making them content and wholly dependent on **Dick-Milk**® [18.13a] as their only source of nutriments.

Make no mistake about the Sissification® program, we're not raising just feminized boys, we're raising an army of mutated non-impregnable, Gurlified® male animals, with real human feminine features to be Whores.

Please get to point Yanket!

Yes, these Whores who will spend their entire lives giving labor compensation sex to horny, yet some would say perverted, hard-working productive men. Let's face it Chairperson, with the worthless value of the US dollar today in the post Federal Reserve Bank (2213) era. **Vaganus**® is the new money. We should be erecting monuments and statues, honoring and worshipping Sissies as our only economic salvation!

Wow! You make a great argument Dr. Yanket, thank you for your meticulous portrayal. But why can't we just increase labor the way, by imprisoning lazy workers! I'm sorry, I mean, indoctrinate the Non-Studs or captured allies and then put them to work in our **FEMA** [4.D-G7.13] camps?

Chairperson let me be blunt. The American empire has lost its once great hegemonic power. And we just can't survive pushing the USA Inc. population into another revolt. Look at it this way, workers won't accept our US dollars anymore so the only thing left is to give them something they're ad-Dick-ted to, Pussy! In our case the United States Inc. has a new set of moral rules and the technology to breed these monkey-cunts who are not just man-hungry, but also by genetic modification, ad-Dick-ted to male sperm. These feminine, well trained pretty little mutants dressed up as girls, Sissified® and Cuntified® with a **Vaganus**®, find it a privilege to be a Sex-Toys for men. This has, in reality, cost the US government a lot less than trying the old morally correct way of world domination through imperialism.

Jizz-Us® Yanket! You said all that in one breath, amazing! (The Chairperson wants his preaching to end sometime soon).

Well, look at the statistics! Unemployment is 69 percent down from 96.69 percent, production levels have not been this high since before all our good paying jobs were outsourced two centuries ago. So I guess we're doing something right! Sure, 69 percent of Non-Stud working class Americans are still considered at poverty level in cums and only eat one meal a day. And sure they live in squalor in a FEMA controlled city or a FEMA detention camp. But hey, now they have running water and one bath a week.

Yes! Look, I agree with you Yanket. And who knows, if the Non-Studs work hard enough they might have the opportunity to have a little bit more hole to penetrate. Hell maybe even legal recreational Prayer-Sex.

Exactly! They could even have hopes of a prosperous and abundant future of an unlimited amount of Sissies like the Stud-Class does. Who by the way, are all on the Penis Enlargement Drug, the **PED** [4.D-G1.8].

Yes, thank you, I agree with everything you've told us Dr. Yanket, but how can we speed up the mutation, transmutation and breeding to increase production?

Well Chairperson, I don't think it's possible, like I told the Cum-mittee, cutting corners on quality, would jeopardize the quality of the Sissification®. But what we can do temporarily is change some of the age limits required for Whores working at the Whoring Stations, at **WS**®.

Great! Let's do it!

Well, this is gonna be hard because my assistant director Seymour Goldberg just came back from a Whoring Station and had his boner fluffed by a six year old and the Sissy Whore who compensated him was only eleven. We're talking humanoid pedophile and animal abuse stuff here. And if they weren't registered mutant or transmuted, **TM**® [2.B2.11] humanoid Sissies I'd be bailing my assistant out of jail.

Whoa! What's going on at the Whoring Stations?

Chairperson, these are hard times! We're just short qualified Sissies. Qualified, meaning old enough to safely take the kind of daily **Cockage**® (Sum of vaganus penetrations) which is estimated as the quantity necessary to service the entire US workforce to sustain the current production levels.

This is a travesty to the Sissydom world! What's going on Yanket? Isn't the Department of Health & Mind Control, the **DHMC** [4.D-G6.1] in control of Whorehouses?

Just hear me out Chairperson. The typical Sissy working at a Whoring Station has to perform, on the average at least three hundred Labor Compensation Transactions, **LCT**s [4.D-G2.27] per shift to meet the quotes of the Sexually Satisfied Male Index, the **SSMI** [4.D-G4.11].

Wow! Okay. Huh!

I know, horrific! But the problem is, physically it's been proven two hundred per ten hour shift of a five day work week is a safe and reasonable quantity of daily **Cockage**® per Whore over the age of eighteen.

So, you can see because of this we're running in dangerous waters here because, the average age of a registered Sissy Whore working at a Whoring Station (WS) is only twelve years old. And the average whoring animal works a fifteen hour shift, six days a week.

For the love of Cock! Dear Jizz-Us®.

Yes, it's sad! We are wearing out these precious little indispensable mutated sex machines. The fallout is proven by the higher than normal medical sick-leave days taken by the Sissy Whores and also by the SSMI® which is down, effecting productivity rates of factory workers. It's a proven fact if an American male doesn't have Sissy-Cunt® to stick his dick into and supply him with an LCT®, they don't work as hard. And hell! Sometimes they just stop working altogether, it's pathetic! But, no transaction, no work!

It sounds horrible Dr. Yanket! Just image the stress caused your Assistant when he found out, the Whoring Station was improperly staffed which could have led to a dissatisfactory service to his manhood! This kind of inconvenience is deplorable! And hey! Despite the triviality, I'm glad our hard working little Sissy-Boys derive increased sexual joy from the pleasure of being screwed in the ass, I sorry I mean, Vaganus® more frequently.

Yes, yes Chairperson! And not to mention their sore little bottom-holes, ouch!

Yes Yanket, it sounds like they're getting the abuse they deserve and crave. Of course it goes without say they willingly bend over, so naturally they're going to have sore Sissy holes. Besides them being programmed to experience pleasure from abuse.

Yes Chairperson, they're holes are being abused, but oddly enough, there's no shortage of Sissy-Puss volunteering for the extra shifts with additional hours and increased **Cockage®**. I guess once a Whore always a Whore, right?

Haa.. Haaa! Huh! (The entire hearing room roars with laughter). Haa... Sluts! Haaa... hee... haaa... Cum-o-holic..... Freaks! Whores! Ha... ha... Haa... Scanks! Heee... ha....

YEAH! We are Whores! And we have RIGHTS!

Thump, Thump… Miss you're out of order! (The Chairperson slams the gavel down).

NO! This hearing is out of order! You're all a bunch of Sissy hating HYPOCRITES! You're BIGOTS…!!!...

Shut-Up… !!!...

Shut-Up you freak! You Whore! Get out of here you fuck-monkey!

Order in the Cum-mittee room! Order in the room! (The Chairpersons gavel slams down on the desk again). Thump, thump, thump...

Calm down folks! Miss I'll have to ask you to please leave the hearing room.

I'll leave when Cunt-gress passes the Sissy Civil Rights Act! That's when I'll leave! When I'm a Free Sissy!

Okay! Officers, please escort this young Sissy out of the Chambers, thank you.

Wow! Unbelievable! I guess some Sissies have more up their ass than hard cock!

Your right Chairperson, I mean the gall of this Sissy. They have more dick than they can ever provide compensation to. All the cum they can swallow! They have a roof over their heads, a government who not only created them but also cares for them as well. Huh! And this is the kind of gratitude we get. Pssss!

Yep! Well Dr. Yanket they don't understand it's the American way, some of us, well actually 69 percent of us just has to bend over or capitalism wouldn't exist. Look, at any rate, their obstinate behavior and their sore holes are of little concern to me. The issue is, we have to and must provide an adequate amount of fresh hole for American workers to enjoy, so we can make the productivity go up. Like I was saying, our real problem is worker productivity.

Ahhh... Well yes of course. Getting back to our problem, I have only one solution to our lack of qualified trained Sissy-Cunts.

What's that Dr. Yanket?

To reduce the amount of sick-days and their hole soreness we can increase the size of their Vaganus® holes through a medical procedure called the, Compensation Orifice Widening Procedures. The **COWP**® [4.D-G1.2] is necessary only because of a bio-engineering flaw in the genetic modifying Sissification formula which does not provide the mutated Sissy child with a wide enough Vaganus®. See Section 4 of Appendix D,

SM069, Table D-G1: Medical Procedures & Drugs

Geeeezy Weeeezy! You mean to tell me the mutant Sissy animals are born into this world with the same tight little asshole as the humans? My God-of-Cock! This is a serious design flaw!

Well yes I agree Chairperson, but currently to solve this imperfection in the mutation, the humanoid Sissies are required to have their Vaganus® holes widened by the COWP once a year on their birthdays.

Huh! Shocking! What the hell is going on here! Your Sissification® program sounds like a sham illegitimate operation!

NO! It's legit! Physically, we can do the procedure to them every four months without any physical harm to their precious Vaganus®. This way those little man hungry, labor compensation sex machines can stay on the job more hours and handle the amount of **Cockage**® we need them to perform.

Wow! Okay Dr. Yanket, I guess as long as the quality of the labor compensation transactions, the LCT isn't compromised, I think we have a solution. Younger Sissy monkeys with wider **Vaganus**® holes. Go figure! Huh…

Yes, yes, this will definitely work! We'll schedule the Sissy

Whores who have more COWP to handle the larger Stud-Class Alpha-Type managers and the ones with less COWP to service the less superior not so endowed, lower class Non-Stud grunt workers.

Thank you Dr. Yanket! It sounds good. Well we're out of time today but let's implement these changes and discuss the progress at the next Sissy Breeding Qualifications and Management hearing.

Thump, Thump… (The Chairperson slams the gavel down to conclude the meeting).

Chapter: 3 Family

[3.1] BREEDING FAMILY

The year is, 2232...

Damn these forms are a million pages long!

Yeah Honey, it's about the size of this erotic political satire novel I'm reading from that Chinese-American chick, Sue Yan Nish. (Sam shows Sandy the book). And I bought the manual too, look.

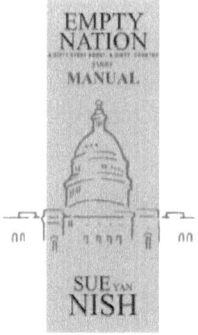

Oh yeah it's a thick book! What's it about?

About how our Neo-Fascist governments hides the truth about how it exploits USA Inc. citizens for profit. Ouuugh! I bought it used and there's a cum stain on it! Geeezzz...

Hmmm... Must be a good erotica story if the previous reader needed to getta load out!

True! Haaa haa ha... Ahhh... (Sam browses the book while trying to wacking-off his tiny little peanut sized Willy). It's a very juicy story! Ahhh...

Well whatever, these questions on the form are be cuming increasingly complex. Hell the Sissy Family Application (**SFA**) [4.D-G5.4] is gonna take forever to fill out!

Yeah Sandy, the **SFA69** form is huge!

Sam Baby it's worth it. Just think about how happy we'll be breeding and raising our **Sissy**® children.

Hmmm… Mwah… Can't wait Sweetheart. We'll have a dozen of those horny little creatures. It sounds like a dream cum true. God-of-Cocks, I could ejaculate in my panties just thinking about it!

Yeah Sam! Mwah… It's the American dream. I didn't realize how beneficial it was gonna be to be from a family where all the males had mini-dicks. Heck, it was well worth the humiliation even though it was sexually depriving at times.

How so Honey? You weren't satisfied?

Well Sam, All my girlfriends in school would brag about how they were getting laid.

Wow! Sounds rough. (Sam is still stroking his peanut with his thumb and forefinger, hinged on every word of Sandy's naughty childhood story).

Yeah it was! I can remember being made fun of in high school because all the girls knew my effeminate brother had a pinky finger sized dick, not much bigger than yours Sam.

Wow! You know I was bullied in school too because of my size. This was when I started wearing girl cloths.

Honey this was only part of the story. At home, the incest sex when I was growing-up in my family sucked!

Ahhhh… Baby! Mwah… You poor thing.

Sam, it was pathetic none of the tiny little pricks in my family could penetrate my tight little virgin pussy. And you know me Sam? I've always been a bitch-in-heat, talk about disheartening.

Ooooh! Mwah… (Sam hugs his wife Sandy to console her).

Yeah, by the time I was fourteen I was so desperate from not getting any dick at home, I was screwing everything in sight, neighbors, priests, teachers, strangers, broomsticks, anything! Hell! I was hanging out in men's restrooms.

Ahhh… Poor Baby! You couldn't get any sex at home?

No! No! I'd parade around the house naked or in a sexy little baby-doll trying to get laid. But got nothing but an anti-climactic pseudo-intercourse, where the family dude would end up dry humping me. And typically out of frustration they would just jack-off and spray their Jizzies onto my invitingly wide-open and dick craving cunt.

My gracious! No Cock! Ahhh…

Yeah, yeah! They never filled my lovehole with their Man-Cream®. Which would account for why I became the slut I am today, right?

Honey, I love my Slut-Wife. Mwah… Mwah…

Mwah… But heck, Sam now we have each other to love. I'll be soooo happy if we're approved for the **SBP**. I just want to start a Sissy® family where everyone loves each other.

Yeah Babe, we'll have lots of love in our house. If we both get approved for the Sissy Breeding Program (SBP) we can breed Sissies like rabbits, cost free! We'll have Government paid housing, a daily supply of freshly bottled Man-Milk® Sissy-Food®,

Yep! And a Live-In Sissy Trainer (LIST), maid-service, free transportation, Sissy medical coverage and college tuition at any Integrated College of our choice.

And for the Sissy-Husband, a job at a Whoring Station, all Sissy expenses paid. What a life Sam Goldberg! I'm so glad I'm married to such a wonderful Sissy kinda man like you Hmmm... Kiss.... Kissss. You're the best Babe!

Sandy the amazing thing is, your cousin Seymour Goldberg started the whole Sissification Program.

Yeah Seymour that horn-dog! That was a great threesome we had when he met-up with us on our Honeymoon.

Yeah Seymour is always horny, but a real gentleman. He just had to do the Bride! Remember he asked you for permission to cum in your Brides pussy.

Yeah, I don't know why he asked, I told him you were a dirty creampie whore. But hey, Seymour's such a nice guy.

Sam it was a great time with Seymour, so romantic. The best wedding a girl or gurl could hope for! But you know the size of Seymour's dick and this is what has me worried about our qualifications. Are you sure about the penis sizes in your family? I mean my cousin Seymour has a bigger weenie then you do. But it's below average at only four inches. This makes it just slightly bigger; I'm talking millimeters bigger than the maximum penis size for the Sissy Class. Do you see my point?

Yes Sandy, I know the Sissy Class cocklets in the MSES all need to be three inches or less. But look Honey, the men in my family, the Boosh family, are all small and totally queer crossdressing faggots. And they all have an acceptable POLC rating except for maybe Seymour. Huh I don't know any male relative who hasn't tried to jump me with their tiny little pecker and succeeded.

Ok Babe, yeah I've been to bed with all of your family too. I know they're horny, I get it, but it's not about queerness it's about penis size Sam.

Yes Baby, but you know I swing both ways, I've sucked and did it with every guy on both sides of my family, uncles, cousins, nephews, grandfathers, my dad, they're all under three inches, believe me.

Hmmm...Kisss... I believe you Sam Honey, kiss... And you know I love you no matter how small your cockette is. You're my little Sissy husband Lover forever, hmmm....kisss.

I love you too Sandy from the time you sucked me off at the Sissy-Rights protest. You didn't care that my dress was torn open and my lip was bleeding after I fought with the big homophobic, Sissy-hating, macho, asshole Cop.

Are you kidding Sam? I fell in love with you that day. You're my wonderful brave Sissy-man; I love you Sam, hmmm, kiss... I don't care if my Sissy man has a tiny little pinky size boy-dick. You're still my man, kisss… Kisss.

Sam, you make love to me better than anyone has ever loved me regardless of how big their pricks were. And you know I'm a big-time gangbang whore. I've done thousands of guys in my life, and even had foot-longs pound my cunt. But Baby, you're still the best lover I've ever had, you and your precious little three incher. And where in the world would I ever get another

Cuckold Sissy husband like you to eat out my cum-bucket after I get gangbanged? Hmmmm... Kisss, I love you Sam Antha!

Kiss, I love you too Sandy Honey, we're the perfect whore couple, hmmm.... kissssss...

Six months and nine weeks later…

Honey, Honey, look what came? Oh, my god it's from the US Department of Health and Mind Control, Sissy Breeding Division, the SBD.

Open it! Open it! Oh god of Cocks! I hope we're approved!

Well, I know they did their homework; my uncle was arrested for not showing up for a Penis Official Length Certificate validation, a POLC appointment. It's the mandatory penis measuring appointment. So I know the folks at the SBD were trying to verify our qualifications.

Ok, Ok, open it already! Ok this is it Baby, You have been,

APPROVED

YES! YES! YES! We're in! YES! Happy days Baby! Whoo hooo! We're approved!

We're in! Honey we're in!

Whohooo! God-of-Cocks! We're in! Let's breed those little man-pleasing Whores! Oooh! Knock me up Baby! Screw your Sissy breeding bitch! Now baby breed me NOW!

Honey you realize it's because we're humans that we need to be inoculated first with the mutating drugs to produce a Sissy baby?

YES, Yes... I know! SLAP! I know Bitch! Slap (Sandy slaps her Sissy husband hard in the face). Just do me Sam!

Ok, ok... Ow! (Sam is holding his face).

Bend over Babe! Aaaaah! Thump, thump, slap, slap, thump. Aaaah! I'm trying Babe! Agh! Wait! What if we have a girl, a human girl?

Oh Baby! Just keep going! Don't stop.... Aaaaagh! Ahhh...

Well a girl would be even better; human daughters in a registered Sissy Family ain't bad. Aaaagh... Can legally have Incestual-Sex. Aaaagh... This means we can breed even more Sissies! Aaaagh.... When she grows-up she'll be cums a Sissy Breeding Female, an **SBF**® [1.A2.3].

But, but... Huh, huh, huh... (Sandy is panting hard). We always have to follow the rules Sam. Studs® visiting a Sissy Family Whore House, **WH**® [7.G4] Aaaagh... can only do the Sissy Family females in the ass.

Yeah, yeah Baby! In the Human Female Anus, the **HFA**® [4.D-G3.16].

Right! Ahhh... Right! Ahhh.... I guess it keeps unwanted pregnancies down. I read the section on **Sex-Laws**© [7] in the Sissydom manual. Harder Sam! Agh!

Right Baby! Vaginal Penetration Prohibition, **VPP** [14] is illegal. You know what they say,

  If a man doesn't own it, he can't poke it!

Yeah! Huh, huh... The registered **HFA**® Lady only provides a man somewhere to put it! But a guy needs to be a really **High-Ranking** Stud [5.E2] to have access to a girls backdoor HFA®. Ahhh… Ahhhh… Yeah…

Yeah, yeah, like that Baby! Agh! The dudes Stud Cock Ranking, his **SCR** [5.E2.1] needs to be really high, like a horsecock L12.

Oooooh! Shut-up Sam! Agh! SLAP! Oh!

Yeah please slap me again Baby! Oooh! I love being submissive for you Baby. Spank me! Agh! And only after the Sissy of the house gets, Aaaagh... the first round in a twenty four hour period.

Slap! Slap! Slap! For Cock-God sake! Shut-up! Oooooh bang me! Oooooh! I'm Cumming! I'm Cumming! Aaaagh!

So yeah! Sissy Family parents can get some back-door action too.

Yes, no kidding, all the Sissy-Family members can take it up the ass? Oooooh! Yeah… Mwah… Nice screw Baby! Hmm.... I love you Babe kissss... You're the best... Hmm.... kiss.

[3.2] PLANNING

After sex family planning…

Oooooh! That was good Baby. Mwah… I love you. Ahhh… Sweetheart our Sissy-Family human daughter would be qualified to be cum a Sissy-Mommy just like you Sandy.

Yeah! It's a Sub-Class of the Sissy-Class. A Sissy-Breeder® has a lot of privileges in the new modern society, in the **MSES** [23.13]. With the creation of the, Modern Social Economic System here in the United States Inc. we enable, under strict regulation, the feminized Sissy-Breeding husband to breed with a **Sissy-Family** daughter after her thirteenth birthday.

Right, right. We're legally allowed to **Cross-Breed**® [7.G1.7c] incestuously because the Sissy's are classified as animals not humans. Yeah Babe it's all declared legal in the Sissification Act. Sex with other Genomes is permissible provided they're at least 69 percent human. Because it's illegal in the USA Inc. to participate in beastly sex.

Here Honey, Mwah… Look it's all here in the Sissy Manual SM069.

Mwah… It's wonderful Baby. Our government figured in all out for us.

Yeah, I forgot all about the incest and pedophile **Sex-Laws**® being void for registered Sissy-Class Families. It's awesome!

Right, you know why?

I gotta feeling you're gonna tell if I don't, go ahead! Tell me.

Well, here in the United States Inc. our government is desperate for more humanoid Sissy Whores to be bred. And I agree completely with our government, I mean, why would I not?

You gotta point Honey-Bunny! Considered the Government is the only business left in this Cunt-trie.

Well we need more creatures like Sissies to do their civic duty for our Cunt-trie by working in a civil servant job. Who else but the bio-engineered Sissies would be physically capable of providing quality sex to all the workers for labor compensation transactions? The **LCT**s [4.D-G2.27].

Exactly Sam Honey, it's even considered patriotic to have two or more Sissy-Breeding females in a Sissy-Family. Like a mother-daughter pair of Sissy breeders.

Hey! We human Girls have to do our part in the **MSES**®.

Ah huh! Sandy, our Sissy children can breed Sissies with you too after the Sissy's thirteenth birthday. Our Sissy kids can knock-up their human mommy!

With what Sam? Their little pinky sized dicks? Sam your DOM-**Cocklet**® [1.A2.1] is long for a Sissy at three inches, but I've seen Sissies with one inch long dicks.

Sure I know, those are **B-Type**® Bitches [1.A2.2] and it's called a Sissy-Clit at only one inch. But we could collect the Sissy Jizzies in a cup or in a tiny little Clit-Sock® condom and use an injector to inseminate you.

Oh! You mean like lesbians do it?

Yeah, yeah Sandy, It's a lot more complicated.

Yeah, it's called artificial insemination. But regardless of Sissy Clit size, we'll be one big gangbanging Sissy-Family! Oh Honey, I'm sooo happy, we're living the American dream!

Yep! Mwah… You realize it's encouraged for all registered Sissy-Family members have sex with all other members of the family?

Oh Honey yes, yes. I know and this is because we live in the best Cunt-tree in the world! Where else but in the good old US of A Incorporated does a government encourage people to have as many Sissy offspring as we can breed. Sammy, I wanna get knocked-up as soon as and as much as I can. I'm so proud knowing my feminine Sissy-Husband can take a gangbang with the same guys who screwed his whore of a wife.

Ahhhh… Only in America Baby. Only in America.

And, Sam you'll get your gay Sissy wish, the father is always the first one to penetrate a Sissy-Baby after birth. It's great, the doctor does the circumcision, and the **COWP** [4.D-G1.2] right there immediately after birth, they start Sissification® from the moment they pop out of the Sissy-Breeding® mommy.

True Honey. Hey, my dad didn't do me in the ass till I was five years old. He lost his job, pension and our house as most Americans had after the Sixty-ninth Economic **Holocaust** of 2210 [23.5.1]. Every company was swallowed up in a hostile take-over by foreign companies and governments. But I didn't care why he mounted me, by then I wanted him inside my ass-pussy sooo bad.

Hmmm… Mwah… Sammy, how did you get deflowered?

Oh, one day after Mom dressed me up in some really pretty girly cloths and had me eating her out, on the bed.

Ahhh… My Cunt-Muncher! Mwah…

Yeah, but then my Dad walked in on us! He just dropped his pants lubed my little bottom-hole and this is how I lost my virginity.

Mwah… You're a good little boy Sammy. Mwah…

Thanks Honey. And granted, you know he has a small little cockette like me and the rest of my relatives, but it was my first time, so it was special. I remember he could hardly get his tiny little pecker up my boy-pussy, but he none the less managed to wiggle it in about an inch. So it was more of a ceremonious jizzing event than a real copulation.

Mwah… Ooooh! My brave little Sissy-Boy! Mwah…

Yeah! Mwah… Still I could remember it was a nice feeling because it was the first time I'd felt a sperm load in my ass and it felt sooo good!

I bet it did! Did you feel **Gurly** Sweetheart? Did you feel like a slutty little pussy? Mwah…

Well yes I did! Mwah… It was warm and creamy. It slowly leaked out and ran down my leg onto the little girly lace-top stockings my Mom dressed me in. Then I just reached down between my legs to my tight little deflowered boy-pussy and pushed my asshole real hard like I was taking-a-shit and the load of my Daddy's love-cream popped out onto my hand.

Oooh! That is so sweet! You collected the Creampie®.

Yeah, I brought it up to my mouth and just licked and licked my Dads Man-Cream off my hand for what seemed like hours. Hmmmm! I was so glad I got to taste my Daddy. I knew from that day on, I would be a Sissy-Bitch.

My good little Whore! Mwah… Ummm… I love you Sammy.

Well, after this deflowering, I became my Dads little cock loving Whore. But only behind closed doors, because back then it was illegal to screw under-age Lady-Boy kids. There was no Sissy transition program. No MSES, no Sissydom, no breeding program.

Well didn't matter you were a boy raised as a girl by my parents?

No! No! It was totally illegal. I'm just glad my parents liked sharing their pretty little faggie Girly-Boy son with their friends.

Oh, how so, Baby? Mwah…

Well, my Dad and his buddies would have card-games where I was passed around. And Mom would have her garden club ladies over to plow my ass with their huge strap-on tools.

Oh! Awesome, Sammy!

Yeah the garden club ladies sowed their feminine seeds in me and watched me blossom into a beautiful Sissy flower.

Oh Sam! Mwah… Thank the God-of-Cocks for modern life and society's willingness to cast-off its bonds of old morality based on religious myths and the first US constitution.

Oh yeah Sandy! And not to mention our American government promotes and legalized incest in registered Sissy-Class Families. As well as building the Modern Social Economic System, the MSES as the framework for sexual equality between the Sissy and Stud Classes.

Yeah Sandy, it's great we'll be one big happy Sissy-Family. Of course our home, which the government provides us, will be an Official United States Government registered Sissy Whorehouse® and we'll have to have open house every weekday between the hours of, eight to midnight.

Well Sam the idea of there being a Sissydom Whorehouse® in the Sissy families home is just to provide sex-training for our precious Sissy kids so they can have all the skills they'll need to be cum professional **Whores**® when they're all grown-up.

Right, right! They'll be in the **Whores-for-Profit**® market, part of the Integrated Monetary Fund, the **IMF** [21.6].

Hey! You know me Sandy. The whole **Sissification**® Program has provided sooo many benefits to Sissies and their families, 69 percent employment in a somewhat well-paid secure government civil servant job. I'm so happy and proud to be an American.

And as registered Sissy parents we'll benefit sexually from the Whorehouse, **WH**® as well. Because Honey according to the WH rules in the Sissy Manual SM069, if the visiting Stud® dude has performed his training and has emptied his first load in our precious little Sissy-Boys Vaganus®, then they can have at our bottoms all they want.

Hmm... Mwah... Oh Sammy, I can feel the Man-Cream® leaking out of my hole already. Kissss...

Hmm... Kisss... Ooooh this is the best of times Baby!

Sure is! Oh, and hey Babe, stop calling them, Sissy boys. They're called Sissy-Gurls.

Sorry Honey, you know how Non-Transmuted, Non-Breed adult Sissy-in-Training, **SIT**® [1.A2.4] Sissies like me are.

Yeah Honey, you Non-Breed type Sissies don't know what-the-fuck you are! But our little precious Sissy princess baby is going to be all GURL! She'll be a Pure Breed-from-Birth Sissy, a **BfB**® [2.B2.12]. Sandy Honey, I love you! Hmmm... Kisss... I'm sooo blessed you're in my life. Mwah...

Well regardless of from birth not from birth, there're only few real differences between a human female girl and a SissyGurl (1) the Gurl® is a patented product of the USA Inc. (2) the Sissy Gurl® has a tiny little pee-pee and a dormant baby making vagina. And also think of it this way, a Sissy has two loveholes, a female has three loveholes.

Ok Samantha Babe, Kiss, thanks for the biology lesson. Mwah…

Oh cool! In the packet that just came with our approval is our Whorehouse number, a Whorehouse rule book, a Sissy Manual and Breeding credentials.

Oh yeah! And it has a poster sign we need to display in the front window so people know we're an Official **Whorehouse**®.

Yep! We're, Whorehouse number: **WH33969R**. What's the R mean?

We're a restricted Whorehouse®. Only Stud-Class men with a Sissy Training Certificate, a **STC**® [4.D-G4.3] can mount our registered Sissy-Whore kids. In other words, the dicks who show-up are not only big but have also been trained how to safely have sex with young Sissies.

Well, we'll be here supervising anyway.

This reminds me Sweetheart. We have to buy a red light bulb for the porch light, so we can let people know when the Whorehouse is open.

Right, we turn the red light on and make sure all of our ass-pussies are douched-out and we're dressed-up sexy for the four hours of sex training by the STC Studs. And we have to be here to supervise the Whorehouse making sure the Sissy Code of Whoring Ethics, the **SCWE** [15] is followed.

Oh yeah, and this includes, NO titillation, this isn't a brothel and it's definitely not a business, we're just doing our civic duty.

Right, our Sissies follow the strict SCWE code, which is in the Sissy Manual SM069. And it's also illegal for a Sissy to solicit, allure and or in any way encourage men to have sex with them, sub-section 15-69.

Exactly Sam! The Sissy Illicit Titillation, the **SITR** [15-69.0] was enacted to maintain the moral fabric of the MSES.

Yep! I read the SM069 and our Sissy children will be a United States Federal Civil Servants not prostitutes. Although it's hard to distinguish between the two sometimes, heeee heee haa ha....

Oooh Sam, you crack me up! I mean the shear thought of our children being considered to be prostitutes is so ridiculous. Hmm.... Kisssss. We're living the new American dream.

Right Honey! Just because humans here in the United States Inc. breed livestock to perform sex with workers, doesn't mean we have a lack of moral responsibility. Hell we're the only nation in the world who practices Cockolicism!

True! But Sandy from what I heard this might be changing!

Oh yeah maybe over the years, the other Cunt-tries might wake-up to the Vaganus® being the only hope for world peace.

Yeah Baby, remember,

World peace through Vaganus® Worship

Hey I just ignore all that old morality bullshit. Americans have new morals now! Like when I think about all the juicy side benefits of a Whorehouse, I salivate.

Yep! Think of all these Studs® being up for a second round of action. We, the Sissies parents can be the happy recipients of their still erect Man-Tools.

God-of-Cocks! My SIT® bottom-hole puckers just thinking about big hard young Studs thrusting in and out of me. Hmmm..... Ooooh! I can have an orgasm just thinking about it!

Jizz-Us® [9.I3.0]. We're so lucky to be Americans! Mwah…

Mwah… Definitely Baby! And like I said, if the Studs® are finished doing their labor compensation thing by training our Sissy GURL, they'll be more than well cum to have both of our bottoms. Mwah…

Right Baby! They can't have at us till they're done with our Sissy-Gurls or if they're feeding her and emptied their ball-sacks into her hungry mouth.

Yep, those are the registered Whorehouse® rules. Mwah…

True we're only going to get second rounds. But you know how the young Sissy sex trainers and feeders are, there's just more chances of getting laid.

Yep! The young Stud® kids can reload really fast because they're all on the Penis Enlargement Drug, the **PED** [4.D-G1.11] medication. It keeps them super hard and horny.

Oh yeah Sandy! Young Studs always have a few loads.

[3.3] PATRIOTISM

Patriotic Prostitution…

Sam don't you think it's odd, it's been illegal for human women to be involved in prostitution after Cunt-gress passed the Sissification Act back in 2213. But because I'm a Sissy-Breeding woman, I have all the privileges of running our very own Whorehouse® right out of our home.

Well yeah, yeah, Sandy, but this is America! We're the innovators, the inventors, and the ones changing the world. We're the ones redefining morality which was based on the old dogma of myths and the antiquated first US constitutions.

Oh Sam you're so smart, kiss... kisss... I love when you start talking stink about the old America! Kisss...

Thanks Baby, love you too... Kisss... If American history tells us anything, it tells us, as long as you have a lot of guns, people will believe, I mean forcefully believe, in anything! I think it's called Imperialism.

Well whatever! Americans are smart. Hell where else in the world can 69 percent of the Cunt-tries population proudly be involved with a service industry devoted to labor compensation through providing sex to workers? Nowhere! Only in America Baby! I mean it's the perfect relationship, our government is our Pimp and we're its Whores, its perfect! In every way!

Oh Sandy I hear you Baby, I'm gonna love watching my wife having sex. You're so patriotic! Mwah…

Oooh! Yeah Honey, sex is so fantastic when we're face to face and both taking it in-the-ass at the same time!

Oooooh Honey, it was so great in our wedding ceremony when we took our marriage vows while we were both taking it in our bottoms. Oh my Cock-God! You're a Girl-Bitch. I'm a Boy-Bitch, what can be better than this?

Ummm… It was so wonderful! Kiss, kiss...kiss. It was the best Cockolic church wedding a couple of whores could have ever had! Our wedding reminds me of all the new Sissy friendly churches in the area.

Oh yeah! Honey if we really get hungry for man sausages, we can join a Holy Cockolic Church, an HCC, there's one about 6.9 blocks away from here.

Right there's an **HCC** [9] a few blocks down on Sperm Street. It was the old broken-down Catholic Church, the Blessed Sacrament. It flipped to Cockolic after the HCC did a hostile takeover of Catholicism.

Ah huh! After the takeover, I think they changed the name. Now its the Blessed Sissy Lady of Cock-Whores.

Right, I heard the Cockolic Church is very Pro-Sissy, Pro-recreational sex. And they promote Sissy-Breeding and Sissy-Incest in Sissy-Families. Also there's prayer group sex with Gurls®. The Sissies are so blessed to be used as cum-buckets to collect the Sperm donations from the parishioners.

It's so awesome Sandy! It sounds like a great place for Sissy family members to get laid both spiritually and physically.

Ah huh, our life is so overwhelming. There's so much love in our lives now. Mwah... I'm pretty sure there're restrictions on, low in cum, Non-Stud working class families, right?

Yeah, yeah well, those poor people can't even belong to an HCC, nor have Incestuous-Sex legally like us Sissy Breeding® folks.

Right, all those poor folks with low or no Cock Ranking Privileges, **CRP** [5.E2.2] are banded from the Church.

Honey! This is all justifiable. Our Founders thought all this through when they crafted the MSES for the new America. Not everybody has privileges in the USA Inc. Vaganus® is the new money.

Oh right Sweetheart! There are only two social classes who survive in this Cunt-tree, Whores® and Studs®, everybody in the middle class is just waste product.

Well hey! I'm just glad as a Sissy-Family we can be open about sex in our modern society and feel free to dress the way we want, screw as much as we can with whomever we want in our cum-munity and family.

Yep! As long as we adhere to the rules in the Sissy Manual developed by the DHMC we'll have a safe and secure future free from having to engage in meaningful thoughts.

[3.4] MCA

I totally agree Honey. We're so blessed. It's all thought out for us in advance. And thank the Cock-God we don't have to do any more serious thinking. Our future is all planned out by the Department of Health and Mind Control. Can you imagine how chaotic the United States of America Incorporated would be if people had to think? I mean, mindless is the new genius.

Yeah! Heaven forbid! Thought is passe in America nowadays. And Sammy, no more behind closed doors, closet sex or politics anymore. Our Cunt-tree is be cuming so free. I mean I feel so free not having to make any more decisions!

Right Sweetheart! We just have to focus on the Recommended Dietary Allowance **RDA** [4.D-G1.29] the nutritional Sperm Intake for Sissies and Breeding families.

Yep! Don't forget the opioids are awesome too! Everything's so wonderful, thanks to the Mind Control Act (**MCA**) being enacted back in 2169 we don't have to waste our time having frivolous thoughts anymore like, how much money is in the bank? Or will we be penetrated enough? Or can we have sex with strangers?

Oh yeah Hun! The MCD medication is really working well! I haven't had a meaningful thought in ages!

Right and as far as us both being whores, I knew when we got Sissy-Breeding married, with the right amount of medication and horniness, we would make it work. Just think, two married whores legally making Sissy-Whore® children and being paid to do it!

It's just un-fucking-believable! Only in America Baby, the land of the free Worker-Studs and the home of the brave Sissy-Whores!

Ten Months later… the year is, 2233...

[3.5] BIRTH

Jane is born…

Waaah Waa Waaah Wah!

It's a boy! Or girl, aaah, I mean Sissy! Congratulations! (The Doctor can't figure out what the heck it is).

Thanks Doctor he's so beautiful!

Yes, he or should we be saying she?

Well Doctor he's not wearing a dress yet but that's the idea (The delivery nurse clarifies the gender question).

True, but I've delivered a lot of Sissy-Boys and this one looks like a perfect little Whore® to me. That's gotta be one of the smallest dicks I've ever seen! For a moment there I thought he

The first of many, times your little Daddy Cocklet is going to visit her Sissy lovehole.

Okay Sissy Mommy and Daddy. Pass your little Whore® over to the Veterinarian so he can pop his load into your new-born Sissy®. Then the doctor will sign the Sissy certificate and the Department of Agriculture's livestock birth record. That will make her officially a Certified Mutant Sissy in Sissydom of the **MSES** [4.D-G2.1] and the property of the USA Inc. government.

True Doctor, the thirty-third **Amendment** [17.33] states All Whore-Class B or D type Sissies are and always will be property owned by the USA Inc.

Holy Cock-God they look so human! (The Doctor is still scratching his balls about the Bonobo Childs resemblance to humans). Huh! I can't even tell the difference except for the little monkey tail.

Thanks Nurse and thanks for fluffing me up for the deflowering.

Sure Sissy-Daddy, it was easy, at only three inches it was really just like sucking a giant clit. I mean I didn't have to deep-throat you or anything. Oh, cum here Daddy let me swallow your little cocklet and balls and clean you up. Your cum load is all over it.

Aaagh! Slurp, Gak, Guk... (The Nurse sucks and slurps Sam). Ooooh! Yeah! Uooooo! Mwah...

Wow! You popped another little load! Ummm... Your daddy cream is so sweet. Mwah... Thanks for the load Sissy Daddy (The Nurse licks cum off her lips). Mwah...

One Month later...

[3.6] FEEDING

Honey, Sam, Sweetie, its feeding time.

Cuming, I'll be right there!

Hey! There's our princess ready to feed on Mommy and Daddy.

Are you ready Baby?

Yeah, yeah I'm always ready to feed my Sissy-Gurl with Dick-Milk. Mwah… She is so precious. Mwah…

And I'm ready to feed her Titty-Milk. Janie Gurl just can't get enough milk from either of us. She sucks down every drop.

Umm… Hmm… We made a prefect **Sissy-Gurl** product. We might only be part-owners with a 6.9 percent share in the royalties, but I'm so proud of her! Mwah…

Yep! She is the property of both our USA Inc. government and us. We bred the product now we'll benefit from our labor. The Breeding program is the replacement for the old Social-Security system. And she loves penetration. Mwah…

Yeah, Jane only cries when a limp dick is pulled out of her. Our little Bitch® is a real money maker! Mwah…

Oh Sandy, what can be more perfect than this? Our Sissy-Gurl needs something up inside of her all the time? Jane's a natural Sissy for sure. She has very strong **Bonobo-Way**® [22.19] feelings and desires for sex.

Yep! Truly a Homo-Sis-Sapien Gurl. She's definitely not human!

Yeah! Total Bonobo! But Sam is Jane Natural or just a genetically modified animal?

Honey! Don't talk like that about Janie Gurl. I'm not sure either what she is but she's our miracle, money in the bank. We both love our beautiful little Sissy-Gurl with all our hearts.

Sure Babe and we know how fortunate and blessed we were to be selected to be inoculated with the **B Formula** [4.D-G1.5] Sissification drug, which mutates the baby into a Sissy Bitch®.

Oh yeah Honey! You kidding? Jane is our cash cow! Bitches® bank a lot of money. And hey! It's natural enough for me. Who cares how they modified our Childs genes in a test-tube or if she's registered as an animal? She's healthy and beautiful and this is all we really care about.

I agree Darling. Samantha, I just think it's so amazing how the bio-scientists can create such a perfect living creature who only wants sex. I mean just think about her adorableness? It's so incredible! Mwah…

Yeah, yeah, yeah… We know because of the gene modification she'll grow-up to be no taller than four feet tall. She's going to have a micro-penis, no bigger than a couple of inches or so.

Yep! Jane is a perfect little money making **Whore-Gurl**!

Ah huh! She'll have the features of a child not older than seven years old, so she'll be a cock-magnet for the new sexually liberated men in the **MSES**®.

Oh yeah! In the Second **Cunt-Stitution**, Amendment 29 [17.29] a Stud-Class citizen has an unalienable right to demand a Whore® citizen perform an LCT on them.

Right! Anyway we know she'll have an exceptionally voracious craving for human penis and produce voluminous quantities of Sissy Clit-Cream for the rest of her life. Who could ask for more?

Kissss.... Mwah…

A little while later…

[3.7] FEEDERS

Ding-dong… Ding-dong….

Honey the boys are here to feed Jane!

Oh okay! The kids from the Sissy Family Support Program, the **SFSP** [4.D-G2.4]. Great, send them up and can you cum up here too and fluff them because Jane's still sucking my tits.

Sure Babe. I'll get the door!

Oh and Sam Baby?

Yeah Honey.

You might want to put some girly cloths on, you can use the practice.

Nah! I don't want to scare the Stud® kids away, remember Halloween when I wore the **Hillary Clitcum** [20], costume.

True! Huh! Don't you dare scare these handsome virile Stud boys away!

Got it! And hey! It's summer. I'm only wearing my sexy shorty-shorts hotpants a halter-top with no bra. So I'll just let my shoulder length hair down (Sam is extremely feminine looking, and has zero body hair), and these college boys are gonna have to figure-out the rest.

Sam opens the front door...

Hello! You boys must be the Feeder's from the Sissy Family Support Program?

Yes Mr. **Goldberg**, we're in the **SFSP** [4.D-G2.4].

Well please cum in and call me Sam. Cum in, I don't bit (Sam winks at them).

Well, we actually signed-up to see if we could get to poke some Sissies in the ass. You know some Gurl® action.

Haaa haa ha… You mean, **Vaganus**? Sissy-Pussy is called Vaganus® [14.O1.6]. It's a registered patented product.

Yes **Sir**! Sorry, we all know **Vaganus**® and all Whores® are the property of the USA Inc. We all took a course in Vaganus Economics [21.B.15] at our college.

Wow! You guys learn all this stuff in college?

Yes Sir! The Whore® is used in the MSES to generate Gross Domestic Product, GDP.

Right! And don't forget, **Vaganus**® is only produced here in America.

Yep! Dr. Jamie Goodass invented the **Homo-Sis-Sapien** [18.0.1] in a DARPA [25.26.1] laboratory for the USA Inc. government as a human vagina substitute. Supposedly for the purpose of collecting a fee for sex-service through Labor Compensation Transactions, the **LCT** [4.D-G2.27].

Wow! It's amazing they teach you all this Sissy-Genome stuff in college nowadays?

Yes **Sir**! The scientists think the **Sis-Gene**® [18.9.1] discovery will save the world. But regardless of the Sissy-Science, our parents wanted us to do something for our cum-munity so we ended up volunteering for the, Sissy Feeding Program.

Oh yeah! And hey! The Sissy Feeding Program, the **SFP** [4.D-G2.5] helps the Breeding Cum-munity.

Yeah we're called **Feeders**. I like it. We score!

Right, right, (Sam winks). So what's your name **Son**?

I'm Eddie Lick! This is John Focker and Steve Woodcock (EN14).

Well **Ed** you can get all the Sissies you want at school can't you?

Sure Sam, we're all from Stud® families so we could screw as many Sissies as we want, but there aren't enough of them at our college yet. I mean, all the Special **Integration** [11] colleges for Stud and Sissy students follow the Sex-Laws® and are set-up to accommodate Human-to-Sissy Sex (**HSS**) [7.G1.0].

Oh! How so? (Sam asks).

Well, there's Whorehouse training benches **LCB**® located all over the school in the, cafeteria, gym, locker rooms, boys restrooms, Stud student lounge, health-room, in the offices of the counselors and principles. But there's just not enough Sissy-Whore® Gurls available. The benches are mostly empty.

Oh yeah! I watched something on Fux News about this. It was a report about the Sissy shortages at schools and Whoring Stations. It's a shame.

Yeah, Sam, by the time we stand in line to get our dicks wet in a

Sissy it's time to go to class, team practice or to get on the bus for home or something.

Wow! It sounds like a real Vaganus Economics crisis!

Yeah, Mr. Goldberg, I mean **Sam**, and when you do get your turn at the boy-bitch you've been waiting for, it's usually a really sloppy hole with sticky cum goo dripping out all over the place.

Right (Steve chimes in), it gets pretty messy and the little faggot's hole is wide enough to stick a telephone pole up it. There's almost zero fiction if you know what I mean?

Yeah (John agrees), you can get more pleasure out of jerking off. And half the time we end up pulling out of the Sissies and just sticking our dirty dicks in the Sissies mouth. But the good part is Sissies can milk your dick till your balls are dry.

Yeah, way better than any human girl can! Haaa...haa (all the boys laugh) ha, ha, ha... Yeah! Sissies are professional cocksuckers alright.

You Sissy feeding boys all know Man-Cum® is the only thing the Sissies were designed to eat or for that matter the only thing they want to eat?

Yes, Sir! We know they feed on our sperm loads. Which would account for, why they're always so hungry for our dicks?

Yeah (Steve agrees) you can tell, the human Stud® Breeding female girls aren't as cum hungry as Sissies are.

Well, boys, follow me up stairs where my wife Sandy is nursing with Sissy Jane.

[3.8] PREPARATION

Up in the master bedroom...

Hey Honey! These are the Feeding boys.

Hey Mrs. Goldberg, how are you? (The well-mannered boys all politely say hello to Sandy).

Hey Boys! How's it going? How's it hanging, heee he… (Sandy scopes-out these young Jock type attractive college boys). Ummm… (She blows them all an air-kiss hello). Mwah… Mwah…

Good, we're a little horny.

Oh! Okay, you came to the right place! We'll make sure we help you young Stud boys out with that horny feeling. The Goldberg family has plenty of holes for you to fill.

Sam volunteers…

Well I think you boys need to get ready to feed your nutritious loads into our sweet little Jane's dick-hungry mouth. So, okay Boys! Now let's see how my cock-sucking talent compares to all the Sissy-Gurls at your college.

Holy Jizz-Us! You're a **Dickgurl**®.

WHOA! Whoa! Hold on there Mr. G! You're not a Sissy! And it's illegal to have gay sex!

Yeah! Hey! We're not Gay man! Sam! If you're gay, you should get help man!

Boys! Boys! Wait! I am not… (The Boys are freaking out thinking they could go to jail and worst if caught having Man-on-Man sex).

Whoa! Geeeezy Weezy! You realize we can be castrated? It's a violation of Amendment twenty-nine.

Okay! Okay! Boys, I'm sorry. (Sam holds up his hands). I assumed you would size me up as a Sissy-in-Training because of my long hair and my femininity. I'm sorry! I'm really a registered Sissy in Training. I'm a **SIT**® [4.D-G3.9].

Oh! Ahhh… Okay… (The Boys are looking a little puzzled).

The **SIT**® is a two year program setup for Sissy want-to-be adult feminine males like me. It originally was to recruit Non-Breed from Birth adult Sissy faggots before the **Sissification**® Act went into effect.

Wow! You're a **SIT**! Cool! My dad told me about guys like you.

Yeah! Yeah! I know what you're thinking. I'm queer, so how am I married to a really hot looking sexy lady like Sandy?

Yeah! Now that you mention it. You gotta admit it looks strange! (Eddie says with a puzzled look on his face).

Oh yeah! It's weird, for sure. But, I'm so proud! There's no shame anymore! In fact, now there's alot of Sissy Breeder Marriages, **SBM** [6.E] feminine husbands like me, in the Sissy in Training, the **SIT** program.

Wow! Freaky! (The Boys never heard of this kinda of stuff).

Well I can explain. You see, after the Economic Holocaust the government encouraged American men to be less aggressive, which caused a lot of erectile dysfunction. It caused the Great American Penis Shrinkage Phenomena, the **GAPSP** [23.17].

Still pretty shocking. Sammy, you're saying, you're a Chick with a dick, a Dickgurl®?

Yes! I'm a Chick with a tiny dick! I'm a product of a truly tragic time in American history! But hey! I only have another six months to go before I take my final Sissy exam. And If I pass it I can file a sexual orientation declaration as a Sissy and get sworn in as a fully trained Certified Sissy Whore, a **CSW**® [2.B2.5]. And also as a United States Federal Civil Servant.

Pssss… Weird but great **Sam**! Yeah great Sam. (All the boys congratulate him). Is the money good?

Yeah! You kidding? Working in the Whoring Industry is an excellent opportunity! It's 69 percent of the USA Inc. GDP.

Wow! Really? The Whoring Industry?

For sure **Boys**! And Sandy and I need two in-cums to survive this kind of sexually liberated lifestyle. We're a two income family. My pay-check from the Whoring-Station and what we'll pull in from our little Janie Gurl® here is gonna provide a decent living. Besides, being a **Dickgurl**® ain't cheap, cloths, make-up, hair salons, jewelry and perfumes!

Huh! Yeah, now that you mention it **Sam**. You kinda look like a sexy Femboy but you didn't have a dress on when you greeted us at the door, so I, I mean we didn't want to assume anything.

Well, to tell you the truth **Boys**. I was actually doing a little survey. I wanted to see if you guys would get hardons for me based just on my own feminine looks and flintiness.

Huh! I kinda was digging you! I was checking-out your nipples!

Yeah, yeah, me too. I was getting a Boner watching you prance around in your sexy hot-pants! You gotta nice ass. So **Sam** yeah.

I think you make a nice looking faggie kinda guy. With a skirt and a little make-up you'd be totally passable.

Yeah **Sam**, sorry we freaked-out on you. Me too (says John), you're hot and you're kind of cute for a guy. Wait! That sounded really gay.

Well, thanks Boys, so don't worry. You're not going to be cum all gay and stuff if I blow you?

No! Not at all! Go for it **Sam Antha**.

Sure **Boys**, I know you guys are heterosexual for sure being from Stud families. Hmmm… Maybe I should have met you at the door naked or in a dress. Here, I'll just get out of my cloths now and you'll see my body is be cuming very feminized by the Sissification drugs, (Sam gets out of his cloths).

Wow! Mr. Goldberg, you're hot (Eddie says)!

Wow! Nice feminine body, very passable (John remarks).

Yeah, you're definitely doable Mr. Goldberg (Stevie chimes in).

Please call me Samantha (Sam drops the halter top)

Wow! Nice tits dude! Whoa! Sam you have miniature balls, so you have a big clit not a small dick?

Oh yeah! Really tiny balls and yes. My penis is classified as a **Cocklette**®. Go ahead! Feel free to feel-me-up. Mwah…

Wow! No body hair and nice ass Sam Antha! Ooooh! Cute Sissyed-out body (All the boys start making-out and feel-up Mr. Goldberg). Your tiny little balls are cute too. Mwah…

Okay, so **Boys**! I'll just be my submissive self and get on my knees here in front of all of you handsome Studs.

Yeah, just be your cock-loving self, **Samantha**. Mwah…

And you **Boys** stick your pricks in my wide open mouth. Just fuck my face. Ahhhh! Nice prick Stevie, God-of-Cocks! You're hung! Guk… Gak… Glrck…

Suck it Bitch! Agh…

Wow! (Sam pulls the dick out of his mouth). Now that you all have your dicks out. Damn! You're all hung! Huh! You're all nine inches or more? How old did you **Boys** say you were?

We're all only eighteen years old Sam. Our families are part of the **Stud-Cock**® Breeding Program, the **SCBP** [4.D-G2.12] to breed Alpha-Males.

Ooooh! Okay, this would explain the large penis sizes of you handsome young men. I was reading about the SCBP, it was started a couple of years after the Sissy Breeding Program. Now that the government knows how long everybody's penis is they wanted to make a super breed of workers and soldiers with foot-longs. The program was started in part by the US Department of Defense (DOD) right?

Yeah, our Dads are all Officers in the service, stationed at the Fort **Didher Army Base**. They're in a special regiment called the 12th Elongated Special Forces (**ESF**). Where all active duty personal are12 inches, 30 centimeters or longer. [25.2].

Okay, I heard one of the effects of the Stud Breeding Program is after an initial period of time the Stud drugs alter the sperm production of the Studs, is this true?

Yeah **Sam**! We're on the Penis Enlargement Drug, the **PED** [4.D-G1.8] and we're all able to produce copious amounts of Man-Cream® now. We even bottle it!

Wow! That's alot of Dick-Milk!

Yes, **Sir**, we produce at least eight, 6.9 oz. loads of Stud **Jizz**® per 24 hours. So the Sissies® are like toilets for us.

Wow! Over two pints per day? It's a lot of pure Stud-Jizz! I mean, as a registered SIT® I drink at least twice that much a day! It's an impressive volume!

Yes Sir! After we signed-up and started taking the PED for the SCBP, and the SFP, we had to start jerking-off into SSSM container bottles a few times a day just to relieve the pressure in our nut-sacks.

SSSM?

The Sissy and Stud Sperm Management or **SSSM** for short [4.9]. It's a Federal law designed as a guideline for the proper storage and disposal of Sissy and Stud sperm.

Right, right, we studied this in SIT class.

But now that we've all been through the Sissy Feeding Program, the **SFP** [D-G2.5], training and are Sissy Training Certified, **STC** [7.G1.1], we can just show-up for a Sissy-feeding appointment and empty our balls into a Sissy's eagerly waiting mouth.

Well you handsome Boys are always well cum here in our Whorehouse®.

Thanks Mrs. Goldberg, and maybe if we have time to reload and the Gurls® parents are up for it, we usually mount the Breeding parents.

Oh yeah! We're always in need of popping off another load or two. Aren't we Boys?

Heck yeah! Yeah! Yeah! (The Boys all agree about extra recreational activity).

Well Boys, let's first do the feeding and we'll see if you're still up for more action. (Sandy winks and blows kisses at all of them). Mwah… Mwah… Mwah…

[3.9] UNLOADING

Stevie…

Guk, Gak, kiss, Mwah… (Jane slurps and licks at the erection in her face). There you go **Stevie**, you're aroused and ready to pop your load, go ahead and gently slide your beautiful piece of young man-meat into the hungry mouth of our tiny little princess.

Gentle! Be very gentle. I take it this is the first time you **Boys** are feeding a little Sissy?

No, **Ma'am**! We've feed quite a few Sissies. We do it at school all the time too.

Okay, well, then you all have experience? Mwah…

Yes, **Ma'am**, we all had to study the Sissy Manual SM069 and pass the **STC** [7.G1.1] exam. Mwah… Mwah…

Okay good! Then you're all STC but please, let's just be careful. And you're not going to stick it down her throat, just gently put only the tip of your dick on her tiny little lips and there you go.

Ooooh! God-of-Cocks! You weren't kidding, she's super hungry.

Oh, yeah! It doesn't take much to encourage a hungry Sissy dinner is being served. Like I said, all you have to do is place the head on their lips and they'll milk on it like their sucking on their mommy's tit nipple.

Aaagh! Yeah! I'm going to pop! Aaagh! Aaagh! Yeah!

Good boy **Stevie**! Feed our little Janie Gurl®. Mwah… Good Boy! Mwah…

Aaaagh! I still Cuming! Aaagh!

Here Stevie let me clean it off, (Sandy gladly gulps down the extra Jizzies). Thanks Mrs. Goldberg. Mwah…

Next! (Sandy shouts out for the next Feeder).

John…

Okay, there you go John. You're obviously ready to ejaculate a load of Sissy-Food®. Oooh! Get up close and let her milk you.

Ooooh! Your hands feel so nice Mrs. **Goldberg**!

You like my hands **Johnny**? You like me stroking your beautiful young Man-Cock? Mwah… (Sandy is kissing and licking the young man's ears and neck). Mwah…

Yes **Ma'am**! Ahhh… Yeah….

Well, let me guide this beautiful hard as rock organ carefully and

I'll just gently stroke you so you can shoot your nice big fresh load into Sissy® daughter's mouth.

Aaagh! Aaagh! Thanks Mrs. Goldberg! Ahhh…

Easy **John**, don't put it in too deep, And please call me Sandy. Mwah… Or hey you can call me whore or breeding bitch. Mwah…

Ahhh…. Ooooh! Yeah! I'm almost ready! Ahhh…

Just in her mouth, you shouldn't put yourself down her throat, easy, and just the head goes in her mouth. Okay. There you go! See how easy it is to feed a little Sissy-Gurl®.

Agh! Agh! Agh! I'm Cumming! Wow she's hungry! Agh! She slurps it all up!

Gak, Guk… (Jane attentively gulps and slurps).

Aaagh! Yeah!

Good Boy! (Mrs. Goldberg congratulates the young man for popping his load into Jane's mouth). Now make sure you get every drop out, here let me clean you, Hmm…. you taste… slurp… so good **John**. Mwah… Mwah…

Thanks Mrs. **Goldberg**. Mwah…

Sure handsome young man you guys are always well cum in our bed anytime, especially with those big beautiful young Man-Tools.

Ed…

Slurps… Guk… Gak… (Sam can't get enough and slurps away at

all the available young cocks). Look at me being a Whore® Honey!

Wow Honey! Are you enjoying yourself over there? Yeah! The Sissy training really shows! You're just slurping away at those Fuck-Sticks!

Aaah! Mr. Goldberg, Sam, I'm going to pop!

Okay Eddie, I see you don't need any more fluffing. Oh my, your leaking Jizzies and your fully erect, all glorious ten inches of you. Mwah…Cum feed our Gurl®.

Ooooh, you're right Sandy. I'm definitely ready to pop my load.

Yeah we almost lost your load. In it goes, be careful **Eddie**, Ok, it's in and now just let her milk on you. Now remember, no further, you don't want the poor little thing to choke and gag on it, she's not your girlfriend or mother. According to US federal regulations Sissies don't start deepthroat training till they're much older.

She's so beautiful Mrs. Goldberg, I mean **Sandy**.

Yes she is **Ed**, and Jane sucks like she's milking my tit nipple.

Yes! Ooooh! She's hungry! Oooh yeah! Ahh... I'm gonna pop!

Yes, please feed our Sissy-Gurl® with your young nutritious Stud-Cream®. Feed her with your hmm... kisss... Beautiful super-hard penis Eddie. Give her all the nourishment she needs.

Ooooh! Ooooh Yeah! I'm Cumming! Aaagh! (Eddie spurts out a load). Aaagh! Yeah! So good! Wow what a hungry little Gurl® you have! She swallowed every drop!

Yeah Jane's going to be quite a cock-teasing trap don't you think so **Boys**?

Oh for sure! And I love the way you dressed her up in sexy little lingerie. She's absolutely as adorable as she can be in this tiny little cup-less bra and crotch-less panties. Oh, she's so cute in her tiny little platform shoes and stockings.

Yep! She's our sweet little Sissy princess. We only shop for cloths at the official **SissyWear**® shops. The cloths are just so hot now and they have lingerie for all ages. It's the only place to shop especially now with the new, Total Sissy Exposure rules, the **TSE**© [4.D-G4.14] rules.

What new rules?

Oh you haven't heard? The Sissification drug, SD69 is working sooo well people, mostly Stud Class folks, were complaining they couldn't tell if young girls or ladies were Sissies or not just by looking at them. I mean really, you can't tell the difference anymore. So, they made the **TSE**© dress-code for Sissies. It's all in the new Sissy Manual SM069, I forget what section.

In the new rules, the Sissies can't cover up their gurly Clits or Cockette's anymore and they're encouraged to wear only official **SissyWear**® which exposes their tits, crotch and lovehole. We love this one shop in the mall called **Pretty-Sissy**©. It has different sections with cloths and accessories by age group. Like for Janie there's a Baby-Sissy® section and there's a Junior-Sissy, Sissy-Princess and a Sissy-Lady section as well.

Sam Antha likes to shop the Sissy-Lady section there. She's found some really hot sexy outfits at the Sissy store. And she loves the peek-a-boo stuff at the **Victoria Secretions**® [10.7] shop.

Oh! Okay so Mr. **Goldberg** cross-dresses in public?

Sure, it's part of the SIT program. Sam has to put in at least 69 hours a week dressed as a Sissy with a minimum of 6.9 hours in public. The SIT program is very thorough. You can't be a closet Sissy like most of the crossdressing US Senators were before the Second US Constitution.

Yeah, I was surprised you **Boys** didn't figure out Sam is a Gurly-Boy? He's as feminine as a man can be. Just look at his long finger nails. Long eye lashes.

Well, yeah, he's very effeminate for a guy. I just thought he was a queer motherfucking bisexual. You, you never know nowadays!

Yeah well she's going through the Sissification® process with SIT program. She takes the Sissification drug SD69, and goes to Sissy training at the local Whoring Station.

Sandy, so if Sam didn't go through transmutation, the TM® process at a **FEMA** [4.D-G7.13] camp and he, I mean she isn't a mutant Breed-from-Birth, a **BfB**, then, what or who is Sam?

Well Sam Antha is what is classified as a **Sissified**®. They're modified by drugs only because when they were accepted into the Sissification Program they were too old to be transmuted.

Wow! Freaky sex change!

Oh yeah! Super freaky, paranormal stuff! You see the Sissy candidate needs to be a prepubescent child for the **Transmutation**® [2.B2.11] to work, if it works. It doesn't work on teenagers or adults. And when the program started Sam was already eighteen and a total queer. So in his case Sam was going to be a Human-Sissy® one way or another.

Well Sandy I can tell the drugs are working and Sam has a lot of experience because he, I mean she can really suck a dick. So I know she's definitely queer by the way she was making-out with my dick. Kissing and licking it like he was in love with it or something. It wasn't just blow-jobs, she was worshipping our dicks.

Sure Eddie the USA Inc. Government's smart. Through the SIT program which is part of the Sissification Program (SP), it provides a Sissy Sex Trainer here at home so he can do Whore training. So we're planning for a total transition in about six months and nine days. He'll have lactating breasts and everything.

Unfucking-Believable!

Yeah! And on her birthday she goes in for her first Compensation Orifice Widening Procedures, **COWP** [4.D-G1.2]. Samantha already has a civil servant job waiting for her at a Whoring Station when she goes total Sissy and is certified.

Wow! Is he keeping his dick?

Oh, yeah, I'm fond of his little pecker. You kidding I suckle on his Cockette® like a tit nipple, except instead of mommy milk it gives me sweet Sissy-Cream. Besides, she's not into the total transgender thing. Samantha still loves what she does to me with her little gurly-dick despite how small it is. Huh! I love my faggot husband so much!

[3.10] PLAYTIME

The boys start to say good bye, but…

Well, **Boys**, I'm glad the feeding went well and please feel free to cum by and feed Jane anytime.

We sure will Sam. We have Jane on our weekly Sissy feeding schedule and we'll also plan visiting during Whorehouse® hours with our parents.

Oh sure! And you boys all know the rules. You can mount me or Sandy only after emptying a load into Jane Gurl?

Yes, **Sir**, I mean Ma'am. Either one of her holes first, got it. Wow! In fact I still think I have a little Jizz left Samantha, would you guys have time for us to pop another load one more time before we leave?

Sure, sure... If you guys think you can go another round. **Sandy**, you up for a little playtime with the boys Babe?

Yeah Honey! Let me put our little whore down for a nap first. I can always use a young hard Stud up my cooch. Okay, you boys meet us in the master-bedroom in a while. Help yourselves to drinks in the fridge.

Okay Sandy, thanks, Mrs. **Goldberg**.

Samantha Honey, why don't you go and get into your Whore® cloths. Put on the new sexy bustier with the garter belt, stockings and a pair of six inch pumps, you know, your Fuck-Me shoes.

Sure Honey! I love wearing my Fuck-Me shoes and getting all Gurly.

Yeah Babe, go get dressed up all Gurly and pretty for the Stud Boys. Then put on a show for us. Oh and wear the pearl necklace I bought for you. And hey Bitch! SLAP.... (In private, Sandy displays a more aggressive dominance over her Cuckolded feminized husband and slaps Sam hard in the face). Don't forget to do your make-up and perfume.

Okay Sandy (Sam says in a submissive voice while batting her eye lashes). Mwah… Don't worry I'll be totally passable.

Yeah, you're so hot when you dress-up I'm starting to see men get hardons just by looking at you Babe. Hmmmm... Kissss.... Mwah… Mwah…

I'm gonna put Jane to sleep and freshen up my ass-cunt a little bit with the **Douche-a-Matic**® machine [4.D-G1.*23*].

Okay, Baby. Mwah… Love you! Oh, that reminds me, I should douche-out for the boys too. We want them to have a nice fresh, lubed-up, Ass-Pussy to plow. Hmmmm.... Kisss.... kisss... Mwah… Mwah…

Hmmm… I do have the sexiest Sissy husband on the block. Despite you not being breed from birth or genetically modified to be a **B-Type** Sissy like our Janie Gurl®. But you're still a hot piece of man-cunt. Mwah… The Boys are gonna love banging you. Mwah…

Thank you Babe, the Sissification Drug; SD69 is really helping a lot, for sure. Check-out my tits they're growing bigger and there's not a hair on my entire body.

Yeah except for your beautiful long blonde head of hair and that beautiful sexy thick pussy bush you have. Kiss me Babe, SLAP!

Hmm… Yeah Baby I love when you slap me in the face! I love being your Sissy-Boy husband Sandy. Mwah…

Love you too Honey Bunny. Now go douche your pussy! Spank (Sandy spanks her husband on the ass).

A while later, Stevie and Sandy…

Knock, knock (The Boys eagerly knock on the bedroom door).

Hey! Cum on in Boys. Hope you guys have recharged your nut-sacks, because I would love to take some big loads up my ass-pussy from you handsome young college boys.

Yeap! Here we are, Bend over bitch, Hoe!

Well, well, a change in attitude young man, from cum-munity minded, Sissy-Feeder to dominant macho Stud dude! Wow! Hmmmm, touch me! Mwah…

Okay, here you go, Kiss... Kissss pop your magnificent man-tool into my quivering backdoor!

Aaagh! Yeah! And I'm in up to my balls deep! Ooooh! Yeah! Oooh! Slap... thump... thump... slap.... Ooooh! Mwah…

Yeah! Do me **Stevie**! I'm in heat, Aaagh! Bang me! (The young man is slamming his prick into Sandy). Do me like you do your mommy! Mwah… Agh!

Ahhh…. I'm Cumming! Agh! Yeah, John is waiting to get on you. I'm done Sandy, Mwah…. Thanks for fuck. Mwah… here Bitch, clean it off. (Stevie sticks his limp dick in Sandy's mouth to get it cleaned). Ahhh…

Gak…Guk… Gek…. Wow! You're hard again Stevie! You and Johnny can just take turns on me! Mwah…

Ed & Samantha…

Wow, Sam!

Please when I'm dressed up I like to be called **Samantha**.

Well, you look hot **Sam Antha**! No facial or body hair at all! Your Baby-Doll looks really nice. Mwah…

Mwah… Thank you **Ed**, am I sexy?

Yes! Yes, cute little tits, petite little feminine body. Definitely hot. Hmmm... Kiss... Kissss. Aaaagh! Sam Antha your dick looks like a big clit and your balls are sooo tiny.

Hmm.... Kiss me. Mwah… Kissss... Oh! **Ed** you're so big!

Oooh! Yeah get on me dude! Mount me! Yeah! I'm a bitch, shove it up me Ed! Aaaagh! You're in! Ooooh! It feels so good! Do me! I want all ten inches in me. Oooh! So Ed do you prefer Sissy-Bitch? Oooh! Aaagh! Or real Girl-Bitch?

Either or Samantha, Sissy or human female. Aaagh!

Actually both Sam Antha, all of us Stud boys do. When we visit a Whorehouse® to feed or to help sex train Sissies, we all swing both ways. I mean, sure I prefer a Pure BfB Gurl® to A SIT. But hey! If the hole is available none of us would hesitate.

Oh! Screw me! Oooh! Yeah! Cum in my Sissy-Puss dude! Ed, please cum in me! Oooh... Shoot your sperm in me! I wanna get pregnant! Yeah!

Aaagh! I'm Cuming! Ooooh! Yeah! It's so good. Aaagh!

Oooh! Agh! I lost my load too without even touching my Cockette®. Thanks for trying to knock me up Eddie. Mwah…

Haaa haa ha… Sure Sam Antha. You're hot for a Sissy-in-Training dude. Especially with the cute little pink bow tied on your Boy-Clit. And you're funny too. You wanna have a baby.

Stevie & John taking turns on Sandy…

Look Eddie, there's my Sissy mommy whore wife, taking it at both ends. And a beautiful sight it is! Sandy has always been like this. In high school, her nickname was Easy Sandy. Actually she likes all her holes filled, my wife's a real Three-holer.

Yeah, **Samantha** and the way she's slurping on John you can tell she craves penis.

Oh yeah! My wife is a total whore for sure and let me share a little secret with you young man, Eddie, there is no better wife in the world to have then one who likes to play with more than one boy at a time. Yep! It's a fact. Whore-Wives are the best!

[3.11] PROMISCUITY

Hey Mr. Ed Lick, Stud Dude! So Ed, what were you were telling me while you were screwing my brains out? Mwah…

Mwah… Oh, about my sexual orientation?

Yeah, can you elaborate for me?

Sure Sam, well, while visiting a Whorehouse®, I like having sex with Sissies and the Sissy family female members. But Samantha, I do understand at no time in a WH or in public, can a male do a vagina unless the male is legally married to the female.

And Sam I know the **Sex-Laws** [7] in the SM069. The United States Cunt-gress passed the Vaginal Penetration Prohibition **VPP** [14] law at the same time it passed the Sissification Act. So it's simple, the reason why males in America screw boys, excuse me, I mean Sissies in their **Vaganus**® is because of the ominous threat of having their penises and balls removed by castration if we break the VPP law.

Yeah Ed, those are the **Sex Laws**, if you don't own the bitch you can't do the bitch.

Right, **Samantha**.

If a man doesn't own it, he can't poke it!

But you know, I was introduced to Sissy-Sex by my parents when I was very young because they didn't want my dick cut-off. They would bring me and my sister with them when visiting a Whorehouse. We were taught and shown, even Human-Sissy Sex, **HSS** [7.G1.0] is not bisexuality or gay because Sissies are classified as females by the, Bureau of Sex Classification, the **BSC** [4.D-G6.4].

Right! And of course this means it's unequivocally true, a Sissy is actually a type of female although not in the same genome.

Ah huh! I mean it's legal for a male to perform sex with Sissies in a Whorehouse®, a Whoring Station or at a Holy Cockolic Church, an **HCC** [9]. All of us, Stevie, John and I have been raised this way. For us have sex with Sissies is natural. Besides it's considered patriotic. We've been taught and realize Sissies were created by scientists in our national laboratories.

Yes Ed, Sissies are an integral part of Sissydom society now!

Right! And those Sissies including a SIT® human Sissies like you Samantha and all of us are part of a liberated Stud-Sissy sexually-free society which makes up the **MSES**.

Heee hee... Yep! One big gangbang smorgasbord.

Forget the old outdated morals the private bankers concocted for profit. The money lenders instill fear into American's through in cum tax, interest rate control and money supply.

Yeah, yeah... Here in America we have a new money system with Labor Compensation Transactions. The LCT done by the **Vaganus**® is all provided by our government owned Sissies. I mean what can be more natural?

And hey Sam Antha, I don't care what they're saying about the USA Inc. in other Cunt-tries. They think we're just a bunch of queers screwing little boy's in-the-ass. But it's not what's really happening here.

Not at all Eddie! Our American version of, in-the-ass, is called Sissy-Sex® and LCT.

Yeah! We have sexual freedom here in the United States Inc. and having sex with what they call little boys is false. The **Sissy**® is a **Homo-Sis-Sapien** [18.15] animal, which looks and acts like a human.

Yep! It's all true Eddie, they look like us but DNA wise, Sissies are no more human than monkeys are. The Bonobo Gene is one of the **Nish Equation** Variables [18.15].

The Sissies are really just mutant humans designed in a test tube to be sex-servants for us hard working Stud-Class American's. I mean Sissies aren't little boys they're a new **Sex-Toy**® owned and created by the US government.

And sure the **BfB** [2.B2.12] Sissies are as tall as a young child and have tiny little miniature penises like little boys, but the bio-scientists didn't eliminate their little peckers through gene modification because they wanted the Sissies to breed more Sissy sex-slaves.

Exactly! Breeding more Whores is important.

Yeah! And in reality breeding is the only benefit of the Sissies having a penis considering its miniature size makes it useless for any pleasurable sexual intercourse. Seriously, I mean our government knows what it's doing. Studs® only bang Sissies for labor compensation and recreation. After all Sissies are just animals.

Yeah but at least they look human! Haa.... haaa.... haaa....

Right, in the MSES a Stud® having sex with a Stud female is for Stud-Breeding only. Sissy-Breeding® mommies and Sissy daughters are only used for recreation and we only screw them in the ass, those are the rules.

Sure Eddie, you're very astute about the MSES. Here I have the Sissy Manual on my night stand. It's in Section 7, Anal sex is always permissible if preparation procedure are followed, **Sex-Laws**® [7], List G1. Human Female Anus, **HFA** (anal only) [4.D-G3.16].

Ed with Sam-Antha…

And, Oooh! What are you doing Eddie? Mwah…

Mwah… Let me show you Sam Antha.

Ooooh! Eddie, you do have a talented mouth. Ummm… Did your Mommy train you? Oooh! And you're rock-hard again. (Samantha has her hands on Ed head) WOW! Do you college boys ever get soft? Hmmmm… Holy God-of-Cocks! It feels sooo good! Mwah… Kisss… Kisss…

Gak… Guk… Gek… (Eddie slurps on Sam).

Oooh! There you go, Aaagh! Swallow every drop, you cocksucker! Oh Eddie, you suck like a Sissy®, now swallow like one! Aaaagh! Hmm... Oooh... Yeah!

Guk… Gak… Gek… Glrck… (Eddie keeps licking and slurping away at Sam Gurl-Clit). Gulp, you're Clit-Cream® tastes so good Samantha!

Thanks Eddie. Ahhh… Yeah… Let me lick my cummy goop off your lips. Ummm… Tasty! I love the way you engulfed my cocklet and balls in your mouth. Ummm… Mwah…

Aaagh, don't mention it Samantha.

You can milk my cum-hose anytime my friend. I love the way you swallow both my tiny little balls and cocklet. Uuuuuuuoo.... You sweet SIT® loving Stud boy. Hmm.... Kissss... Now Eddie, do you feel like a homosexual now? I mean, I used to be a man! And you sucked my little cock?

Samantha, you call your two-incher a cock? Wow!

Well, no, and hey! Its three inches, but you know what I mean?

No, no Sam! I don't feel queer at all. You're a SIT® Sissy and Sissies are classified as females with big Clits or Cocklets, Sissies are just chicks-with-dicks. And no I'm not gay! I'm comfortable with a Sissy cockette or clit in my mouth. No I don't feel gay. Kisss... Mwah…

Well, I'm just checking Eddie. Kisss... Because I don't want to be accused of turning a nice strong virile handsome Stud® into a faggot. Mwah… And I'm not trying to be disrespectful if you are. Mwah…

Yeah, yeah, hey! It's cool. Mwah… Believe me **Samantha** it's not gonna happen. I just love having Sissy-Sex®. Oooh and FYI don't ever call a Stud® a cock-sucking faggot, you'd be asking for trouble. Oh and by the way, I've never sucked on a man in my life.

Huh! Why can't I call you a cocksucker? Haaa haa ha… You just blew me!

Well Studs suck Sissy cockette's and clits NOT Man-Cocks!

Well Eddie, in that case, you're a great clit-sucking handsome young Stud®. Hmmm... Kissss. Thanks... Kissss...

Stevie & John on Sandy…

OH! Yeah! Oooh! Cum in me!!! Cum in my ass-pussy! Spurt your spunk dude! Aaagh! (Sandy is slurping and taking a hardcore banging at the other end). Gak, Guk, Gulp…

Swallow it bitch! Agh! (John is guiding Sandy's head with both his hands). Thanks. Mwah…

God nice load Stud! Thank Stevie for the creampie! Mwah…

Well, I guess they all popped at the same time, what a show!

Yeah nice, very nice. I love watching my wife enjoying herself. They're all just lying there in one big sticky, cummy, sweaty, exhausted, heap of bodies.

Yep! They obviously enjoyed themselves. Sandy my whore-wife, I love you Baby! Do you like to play with boys Baby?

Yes Honey, my loving Sissy husband, your wife is a gangbanging whore! And I love you!

Oooh! I love you too Baby! Hmm.... Kisssss.... Mwah…

[3.12] LEAVING

The boys collect their cloths…

Yes, I'd agree, you are a beautiful whore Honey and the best thing is we're a husband and wife whore couple. Oh and Eddie here confided in me the boys swing both ways at Whorehouses. Heee... hee... he…

Well Sandy, we don't get into dressing-up like a **SIT**® Sissy, like Sam. I mean, when you say, swing-both-ways to us means, Sissy-Sex® not to be confused with Human-on-Human, **HH** [7.G1.15]. This type of sex is lewd and prohibited in the MSES.

Eddie's right. It's just training Sissies and Sissy Breeding women in the Art-of-Sex as labor compensation. Don't take us the wrong way sexually speaking.

Yeah Stevie. None of us take it up-the-ass like Sissies do! And we don't suck penis either, only Sissy Cockette's or Clits. But Sissies are Gurls® so we're not gay. Homo sex and vaginal recreational sex have both been illegal since the Sissification Act and the **VPP** [14] law was passed.

Right! The Vaginal Penetration Prohibition, the VPP.

No, no, boys I know you guys are straight kind of all American Stud boys. I don't wanna convert you to be cum Sissies or anything. It's only for a certain type of person. Not everybody gets feminine feels because they're having Sissy-Sex by sticking their dicks in Sissies. I mean true, Pure American Sissies are part Bonobo monkey.

No offense taken **Samantha**, we love you guys and what you're doing to build an American dominated and controlled Sissydom.

Thanks. What I'm really saying is, it feels good to hear about Stud® families are embracing the new MSES and freely associating with Sissy-Breeding families like us.

Yeah, yeah, I'm thinking it would be great to invite your families over for a, Bar-B-Q and have a good old fashioned **Fuckfest**® with each other. (EN14)

Oh! Yeah, it sounds wonderful Honey, especially knowing how the men in their families are all hung like horses! Hmmm…

Sure Sandy! Our families even have some foot-longs in them.

Wow! Definitely, you boys are from good lines of Studs. Let's get all of our families together for a goodtime. I'll be looking forward to it Samantha and Sandy.

Okay, so we all agree Stud and Sissy families should be friends, share good times and have sexual pleasures with each other.

Certainly! Not just fuck-Buddies! It's all part of the **MSES**® plan to bond Sissy and Stud folks together making a better future for our Cunt-tree.

[3.13] SOCIOECONOMICS

Social & economic issues discussed…

Yep! We're building a pure Stud-Sissy society for a stronger America by being the only nation in the world who supports and condones Human-Sissy Sex, **HSS**®. But in a course on **Vaganus Economics** [22.16.15] the other day, we were discussing the, low in cum, Non-Stud (NS) wage earning workers vs. Stud-Class, bourgeoisie type wealthy citizen issues. The sad part is, Non-

Studs, the NS families cannot have sex outside of a Whoring-Station®.

Ah yeah… But those, poor, lower working class Non-Stud guys are not allowed the fun stuff for a good reason. Stricter sex rules apply for them and they often turn to violence because of sexual deprivation or due to the lower quality Farm Bred Sissy, F-Type, **FBS**® [1.A2.6] Whores.

Well yeah Samantha! Because the SSAAAS keeps track of all penetrations so they can't have sex without the system knowing about it. And they can't engage in Sissy-Sex® or any kind of sex for-that-matter, at home, school, a Whorehouse or even at a Cockolic Church! SSAAAS?

Stevie is right! It's the Sissy Sexual Activity Auto-Accounting System, the **SSAAAS**® [4.D-G1.26]. Nobody screws anyone or anything without the United States Federal Government knowing about it.

True, true. It's all part of the USA Inc. governments big push to have only Studs or Sissies in the **MSES** society. But Non-Studs can use Type-C Whoring-Stations and really those stations are only good for the NS guys. The **Stud** men don't use the C-Type Stations anymore. There're filled with transmuted **TM**®, tranny type **SIT**® and Farm Bred, **FBS**® Gurls.

Oh! Why so? Is the quality that bad?

Well my friend, only scanky Hoe's, transmutant's, Transitioned Sissies and no offence intended Mr. Goldberg. Stud® men prefer pure bred Vaganus®, the **PBS**® [2.B2.10].

None taken. Mwah… But I beg to differ.

I'm a good FUCK… !!!…

Okay! You College boys know, you all had at my bottom! (Sam gets all defensive about his-her femininity so uses one of the flaunting techniques he learned in Sissy training by pushing her chest out then tweaks his nipples to display a willingness to engage in sex). Hey! I'm ready to go again Dude!

For sure Dudette! You're definitely a good piece-of-ass Sammy!

Yeah Samantha! Mwah… Mwah… (All the Boys get consolatory and hug and kiss Sam. They give compliments to her about her man-pleasing quality). Mwah… SIT® Gurls give-a-fuck. Mwah… You're hot Sammy! Yeah Gurl!

Hey! Besides, **Stud**® guys have a much higher Hourly Occupation Male Orgasm, **HOMO** [12.L1.0] pay rank which allows them more sex with high class Pure Bred Sissies (PBS) and at better quality Whoring-Stations.

Right, my Spanish speaking friend calls it, Casas de Putas. The impoverished Non-Studs living in FEMA camps are limited to how much Sissy they can poke. Mwah…

True and in fact. I think they're going to try to eliminate the Non-Stud, wage earning, worker types altogether eventually. Mwah… Mwah…

Well yeah, the robots are eliminating most of their jobs anyway.

Yep! And I heard instead of just performing genocide like the old United States did with low in-cum folks in FEMA camps, they're just going to force them to decide a social direction.

Wow! The middle working class Non-Stud guys are fucked!

Huh! Yes, historically speaking, the working class in the USA Inc. has always been suppressed by the aristocrats. But in modern times these misfortunate working folks were created by the Shrinkage, the Great American Penis Shrinkage Phenomena. Folks were forced into a lower social class due to their inability to purchase enough Penis Enlargement Drugs, **PED** [4.D-G1.8] meds.

Right, right, the **GASP** [23.17]. After the Economic Holocaust of 2007-2008, the government encouraged American men to be less aggressive physically, emotionally or economically.

Yeah, yeah... Well, considering speaking about the GASP is forbidden, just between us, the forced erectile dysfunction by the US government was **Economic Sodomy**.

Hey! Either way, they're being forced into breeding with a Sissy from the Whore-Sissy Class or with a Stud-Breeding® woman from the Worker-Stud Class or the government will just cut-off their food rations.

Tsss... Yeah and in Cunt-gress there's a Society Classification Committee discussing ways of making Sub-Classes for Semi-Sissy and Semi-Stud folks. Mwah... Mwah...

Oh yeah, Mwah... It was on Fux News. If they do this thing called Class **Opt-Out** [13], they would breed outside of the Non-Stud working class and have extra privileges and opportunities.

Hmmm.... But not full privileges until they completely qualify to reclassified into a Stud or a Sissy Class.

Boys, this only tells us one thing. Our Government made these maneuvers before. How so Sammy?

If you look at American history, back in the old Fascists days, the Oligarchy was replaced by the privileged Aristocracy, like Boosh, Clitcum and Trump. The middle-class was just not needed anymore and became a liability to the USA.

Right! I read about this dark period of history. The middle-class was squeezed out of existence. The good quality jobs were sent overseas, benefits eliminated, quality of life controls abolished.

Yeah, yeah… But it's the same thing our government is doing now, the Non-Stud middle, working class is being eliminated!

Yep! Those sick mother-fuckers in Washingcum are increasing the **Race-to-the-Bottom** [23.35]. Meaning the middle-class Non-Studs are screwed!

Why do you think all our dads joined the US Army Sissy Corps and became Stud-Officers? They all traded up to Stud-Class by investing in the **PED**® medication to counteract the penis shrinkage drugs the government contaminated the drinking water supply. Why do you think only Stud® folks can afford pure bottled water and filter systems?

[3.14] GOODBYE

Well guys enough politics! Holy-Poop! Too much information!

Yeah! Besides, the first **Amendment** [17.1] says non-censored speech is illegal. We're not supposed to be talking about freedoms of any kind (Sandy admits regrettably).

Hey! Cum-on, cheer-up! I'm especially looking forward to getting together with your Stud families. Just the thought of getting mounted by a father and son Stud-team has my ass-pussy hole dilating in anticipation. Mwah… Mwah…

Ha haa haaaa! It would be awesome Sam Antha! Well, we have

to get going now. So see you at the next feeding appointment and we'll speak with our folks about the Bar-B-Q aka Fuckfest. Mwah… Mwah…

Mwah…Okay, **Boys**, have fun, save a load for us.

Will do **Sam-Antha**. Hee... hee... ha.... ha...heee... ha... (They're all in good spirits) See yah Sandy. Bye! Bye!

See yah soon **Boys**! (Sandy suggestively winks and blows kisses). And bring your Stud daddies with yah.

Okay! See Yah…

Continued in EN14…

Chapter: 4 HCC

One year later…

[4.1] PRINCESS

Getting Jane ready for Church…

Honey we're gonna to be late for Mass!

Okay, cum-ing, our little **Sissy-Gurl**® is giving me a hard time. What did I tell you! You have to put on your Sunday going to church dress. There! (Sandy slips the Baby-Doll lingerie on Jane). Now let's go princess.

Moments later...

Okay, sorry Babe! She loves to play endlessly with her bunny-tail butt-plug, put it in and take it out, again and again. Agh!

At least we know what's on her mind!

I know right! She just can't get enough of something up her sweet little money-making lovehole.

I finally got her dress on and when I put her baby-platform shoes on she just wanted to parade in front of the mirror!

God-of-Cocks what a glamour queen she loves those platform shoes!

I know! Our little princess loves you dressing her up in sexy Gurly cloths. Which could account for how her total **Cockage**® [5.E1] (The amount of penetrations the Vaganus® has to date) number is so high for a one year old.

Yeah, I swear, our little Sissy-Whore® here is gonna set a record!

Babe, she'll make both of us so proud and not to mention rich! This was the best investment we could have ever made. Breeding Jane will allow us to afford the luxuries in life.

Yep! We sure know how to raise us a hot little money-maker! And she is sooo adorable! Mwah…

Yeah for sure, talk about Sissies. I hear Father Gary is going to start a new gangbang training course for non-breed, non-transmuted, SIT Sissies like me.

Really? Great Sam, its wonderful news for the non-breed Sissy daddies who are transitioning into **Sissydom**® like yourself. More training is definitely needed. Especially for you adult Sissies SITs who converted to Sissydom after the Sissification Act went into effect.

Sure, sure. Mature Non-transmuted Sissies SITs should have the same rights as other pure **BfB**® Sissies do in Sissydom. And going to church reminds me of the prejudices and all the persecuted folks who endure for their religious and sexual beliefs throughout human history.

Yeah Honey, just because we worship Cock as your new God, we shouldn't be persecuted. Our precious little Jane and I have rights to have penises and live and work as **Sissy-Gurls**® for the betterment of our Cunt-tree. When men penetrate either our Pussies we're performing our duty for God and Cunt-tree.

Right, right! Just because Jane was engineered into a non-human existence, she still has the right to worship Cock and be cum a professional Whore-for-Profit. (Both Sandy and Sam are always trying to justify using Jane to turn a buck).

Sure Honey! Just like the wall-street bankers worshipped the US dollar as their God. Unfortunately they also destroyed the American economy and with it the American way of life. We too have the right to worship. To be penetrated by such beautiful things as a man's penis.

I love you Sandy. Mwah…

I love you too **Sam Antha**, you dick worshipping Sissy husband-bitch of mine. Mwah… Mwah…

Sandy you're the best wife a Sissy-Boy like me could ever be owned by. Mwah… Mwah…

Well, my little **Lady-Boy**®, you just keep working at the Whoring-Station and bring me home your pay-check. And I'll give you all the lovin you need Sammy. Mwah…

Jack the Stud Neighbor…

Beep, beep, Hey, **Jack**! (Sam winks at the Stud neighbor Jack Tudiks who the whole Goldberg family has had many recreational sessions with).

Hey **Samantha**, (Jack winks back). You guys leaving for Church?

Yeah, are you guys gonna cum to mass?

Yeah, **Maggie's** getting the Holden ready. We'll be at Church in a bit. (Holden their son is Jane's playmate).

Are you going to stay for recreation prayer group after mass?

Oooh yeah! I wouldn't miss a chance to mount your sweet ass **Samantha**!

Okay, see you there **Jack**! (Samantha winks and blows a kiss at her Stud neighbor) and bring your horsecock with yah!

Sure will (Jack the neighbor whips out his long dong and twirls it in a circular motion), neighbor! Whoohooo!

Beep, Beep… (Sam beeps the car horn back at him in approval of the lewd display).

What great neighbors. Angela and Jack are super-cool couple. And Holden their son and Jane have loved doing 69 in the crib! We should setup more play-dates for the kids.

Sure Sandy! I love when he does both of us.

Oh I know! When he takes turns doing us. God-of-Cocks! What a great Stud neighbor!

Yeah when he pulls out of you and sticks it in me for hours! Oh my Cock-God! **Jizz-Us**® [9.I3.0], the way Jack massages our bottom holes with his man-tool, oooh! What stamina.

What a neighborhood! This is such a great place to start a **Sissy-Family**. We're right in the middle of a quaint little Stud neighborhood with tree lined streets and manicured yards, white picket fences. Fountains with huge phallic penis-looking statues. Everything here is so wonderful, I'm so proud to be an American, Oooh Jane! Ahhhh… Stop munching on Mommies special place Sissy-Gurl.

I know Honey the Sissy-Breeding Program, the SBP is fantastic. They selected a perfect location for our Whorehouse. We're surrounded by Stud Families. And Baby it doesn't get better than this. This is America, the land of hopes and dreams.

Yeah they're all Stud folks except for the **Dune** family a few

Okay Babe, how do I look? (Sam is a little self-conscious about his Gurliness). I'm I pretty?

Honey you're blushing. But, for a cross-dressing faggot Sissy-Boy husband, yeah! You're so adorably cute and you have an unusually high **Cockage**® number. So stop worrying about how pretty you look. Mwah… Mwah…

Yeah, I'll have to go online and check baby Jane's **Cockage**® number tonight.

Really, why? It's not a competition!

Honey I'm just getting a little jealous (Sam frowns).

Ha… ha… haaa… You faggot! You know she'll eventually have a way bigger **Cockage** number than you.

Snifff… Snifff… Yep! Jane will always have a higher Sexual Anal Ranking. Her **SAR**® [5] and the higher Sexual Skill Rating **SSR**®. Snifff… Snifff… I'm just a **SIT**®, just a Sissy-Boy bring home his pay-check. I'm nobody. Snifff… Snifff… (Sam is having a meltdown).

Hun! Stop crying. Mwah… I love you and your pay-check! And Jane is a Pure Breed from birth Sissy, a **BfB**® and face it you're not. Mwah…

Sandy, I'd like to think I'm turning men on sexually. And I can still keep up with the younger more attractive BfB Sissies being breed and the transmuted ones being converted.

Sam Baby, what are you worried about? Your pay-check indicates you're doing fine! It reflects the amount of men who wanna penetrate you for compensation.

Sandy! I wanna attract lots of men to me like you and Jane do.

Sam Antha Honey, men want to hump you too. I can see their hardons in their pants. Men always hover around you and want to get up your mini-skirt! You're hot Baby! Mwah…

Thanks Babe. Hmm…. kisssss… Mwah… Mwah…

And you got killer legs (Sandy runs her hand over his leg).

Oooh Hun! Yeah, you like my legs Baby? How do my stocking look? Can you see the garter-belt straps? How's these pink FuckMe shoes look? I wore the six inch pumps like you told me to. You think the Bishop is gonna wanna mount me?

Oh my Cock-God Sam! You're such Gurl!

Inside the Church...

Oh hey! There's the **Dune's**, let's sit next to them.

Yeah I like **Beth** and **Heather**. Hey guys!

Hey it's the **Goldberg** family, Samantha and Sandy.

Hey Beth, hey Heather (Samantha and Beth both grab each other's clits to do a Sissy-Shake hello). And its precious little **Mary** Gurl! Jizz-Us® Heather she's sooo adorable!

Sissy **Jane**! Mwah…. Wow our kids are so beautiful. Ooooh! Okay Jane, oooh. Ummm…

Chluurp… Chluurp… (The sound of Jane suckling Heathers lactating tit nipple).

Sorry Heather! Jane loves suckling.

It's Okay Sandy. Jane went right for my nipple. Oooh, she's hungry for tit milk.

Heather, Jane's always hungry for whatever, tit, penis, anything to feed off of. How about Mary?

Nah! She's kind of a quiet Sissy has a normal DOM® Sissy appetite for sex.

Well hey! Let's make a play-date for these two?

Sure, sure. It's a great idea seeing how Jane's a Bitch® and Mary's a DOM®, it could be a perfect DOM-Bitch match. Yeah who knows, we might be cum in-laws someday.

[4.3] MASS

(P: Priest, C: congregation, J: Jane, SS: Sam Sissy, SB: Sandy Breeder)

P: Holy! Holy! Holy! Lord giver of sperm, blessed is Cock that cums in his glory.

P: In the name of the Father Cock, the Sons of the Father Cock and the Holy-Sprit of Cock, Amen.

P: The grace of our Lord Cock and the love of God the Cock and the fellowship of the Holy-Spirit of Cock be with you all.

C: And also with you.

P: The Lord of Cocks be with you.

C: And also with you.

P: My Cock worshipping brothers and sisters, to prepare

ourselves to celebrate the sacred mysteries of Cock, let us call to mind our sins.

C: I confess to the almighty Cock, and to you, my brothers and sisters, that I have sinned by persecuting Sissies through my own fault in my thoughts and in my words, in what I have done, and in what I have failed to do. And I ask the blessed Cock, ever Hard, all the Cock Angels and Cock Saints, and to you, my brothers and sisters, to pray for me to the Lord our Cock.

P: May the almighty Cock have mercy on us, forgive us our sins, and bring us to everlasting life with hard Cock.

C: Amen.

C: For you alone are the Holy Cock, you alone are the Lord of Cock's, you alone are the most hard and longest of all Cocks, with the Holy Spirit of Cocks, in the glory of God the Father of Cock. Amen.

Johnny EN01: THE COCK BECAME LIMP

The sermon according to Johnny [9.I6]. Turn to Johnny number 01 in your **HCC Bible** [9]. This Parable describes the Apostle Johnny Jizzing her sinful Bitch then she went limp. Let me remind our youngsters **GOD** (Cockolic Version) [9.I3.9]. Meaning, He-She is either or, there is no gender associated with God. Okay, I'll begin.

[1.1] in the beginning was the Cock, and the Cock was with God the Cock, and the Cock was God.

[1.2] she, the Bitch was with God in bed, in the beginning.

[1.3] through her all things were penetrated. Without her nothing was ejaculated that has been ejaculated.

[1.4] in her was Sperm, and that Sperm was the Holy-Jizzies of all mankind.

[1.5] The Jizz shines in the darkness of the Pussy and the darkness has not over cum Jizz and the Bitch got pregnant.

[1.6] there was a Stud man sent from God-the-Cock whose name was Johnny.

[1.7] He came inside the Pussy and testified concerning that the FEM-Cock® went limp, so that through her limp Cock all might believe her balls were empty.

This was the word of the Lord Cock our God. Amen.

[4.4] SPECIAL EVENT

P: Today we celebrate the special event of a Sissy® Turning One-Year-Old. May the Sissy parents please bring the Pure Breed-from-Birth, **BfB**® Sissy up to the altar for the blessing?

SS: Take the bunny-tail out of Jane's bottom Babe.

SB: Thanks Sammy.

J: Wah! Wah! Wah! Mommy, mommy.

SB: There, there baby Sheeesh Princess (The Priest holds up Jane above his head for the whole church to see).

P: Oh Lord of Cocks, we present to you this day a new Cock worshipper and may through the penetration and acceptance of thy Holy-Cock Man-Cream®, be filled with the Holy-Cock Spirit. Amen.

P: May my Cock blessed by our Holy Cock-Pope® in Roman

keep this Sissy unto an orgasm everlasting. Amen.

P: I penetrate our Sissy Jane, a forever Cock loving pussy with my Blessed Holy-Cock in the name of our Lord-of-Cocks.

J: Wah! Wah! Ummm… Ahhh… Cocky, Cocky… (Jane, seeing the Father's erection whines for penetration).

SB: Sheeesh… Jane Honey, Mommies here, don't cry. It will be inside you soon. Mwah…

P: Holy, Holy, Holy-Cum, the Cream of life, may this Holy Cum load be the Holy-Cream® that anoints this horny Sissy **Sex-Soul**® [21.B.24.2] and well cums her into your Sissydom® forever. Amen.

Aaagh! Ummm… Ahhh… (The Priest gently impales tiny Jane down onto his ordained foot-long prick and after a while fills her with the Holy load) Amen! Aaaaagh! Aaaaah! Yay! Cocky!

P: Ahhh… The Lord Cock be with you! And with thy Cock-Spirit®. Go, the mass is ended. Thanks be to Cock!

P: (The Priests, panting from having just orgasmed, gives the blessing to the congregation) Huh! May almighty Cock. Huh! The Father of all Cocks. Huh! And to all the Sons of Cocks, and the Holy Ghost of Cock, bless you!

[4.5] MASS IS OVER

Oh my God-of-Cocks! Thank cock it's finally over. I'm hard and horny after watching Father Gray's foot-long for an hour. And Father literally banged the Sissy-Poop® out of Jane with his massive ordained man-tool.

My god Father Gary's an animal.

Oh hey **Sam**! I'll be with Father **Tom** I have to confess my sins and do my penance, besides I'm aching to get some Holy-Cream® up my cooch!

Oooh! I'm jealous! Mwah…

I beat you are Honey-Bunny! Tell you what. I won't douche my ass-pussy! I'll save all the creampies for you. Mwah… See yah later. Hmm... Kisss... Kisss... Mwah…

Ahhh… You're soooo good to me! Bye Babe. Have fun!

In the recreational prayer hall...

Ah! Mrs. Goldberg, well cum! I see you setup Jane on a compensation bench, an LCB® for the whole parish to enjoy while in prayer. She is so cute and quite a performer up on the Altar today I might add! (The Father exclaims).

Thank you Father Tom. Mwah…

Yeah she was quite a little show-off up there, she only cries when her bottoms empty.

Yes, yes! And as she should as a follower of **Jizz-Us**® [9.I3.0]. I noticed she was moaning like she wanted more.

Oh Father it was no act, believe me! She always wants more. Jane is a **B-Type** [1.A2.2] so she's hungry for sex 24 hours, 7 days a week, like a good little Whore®.

Well I certainly hope we, here at the Blessed Sissy Lady of Cock-Whores Church, have given your family the guidance it needs to turn a tidy profit from her worship.

Oh Father! I love the way you grab my sinful ass. Oooh! Ummm,

Ooooh yeah! And yes, please continue with every inch of guidance you can offer. We promise the Church will receive a generous contribution from our Janie Gurls booty treasure.

Ahhh… yes! Of course, you will share the Booty acquired from your Cock-Worshipping Sissy® daughter's monetary gains. This is the way of the Lord!

Amen! Mwah… Oh Father, I feel dirty and sinful! Mwah… Please give us your erect guidance.

Yes, yes, by all means. I will cum over to your Whorehouse every Tuesday night, to perform the Sacrament of Holy-Cream Cum-Union® with your beautiful Sissy Jane. It's been a pleasure. So where is Samantha, that SIT® whore-husband of yours?

Oh! He's helping Father Mark. Father did you hear about the new course Father Gary is offering?

Yes, yes, the one on how a non-breed Sissy® handles a gangbang.

Yes Father this one.

Well we're giving the course because of the data the HCC has collected. It's a real problem.

Oh, why so? Mwah…

Mwah… Well we know most non-breed Sissies already know how to handle more than one man in their bed at a time. This is mostly due to the fact that Sissies have an unusually strong sexual desire and have been programmed to copulate countless times compared to normal humans. But it's their hording the Church finds particularly disturbing.

Wow! They horde pricks like Studs in a stable?

Yeah! You see this instructional course is more aimed at training Sissy SIT® daddies to share with the infant and prepubescent Sissy **Gurls**® in their home. We've gathered big-data information on Human-Sissy Sex, **HSS** [7.G1.19] in families for many, many, years.

Father, do you like my peek-a-boo bra? Spy on my nipples Father. Mwah... (Sandy is panting for the Father to rape her, so she opens the top buttons on her blouse and tweaks her nipples for him). Mwah...

Huh! In a moment my Dear. The Church gathered the data through surveillance as had the NSA, CIA, FBI and many other clandestine US agencies in the old United States to destroy the workers rights to privacy, property and or sex.

Wow Father! Mwah... So what did you discover? Mwah...

Well, we've cum to find out, Sissy SIT® daddies often times horde the larger penises in their homes for themselves. Much the same way the banks horded profits here in the United States during the old fractional reserve, fiat dollar era.

Oh Father, I get hot for you. Mwah... You're sooo smart! And handsome. Ummm... Mwah...

Mwah... And the HCC has a simple solution. The daddies just have to be reminded to share penises with the little sex loving children in their registered Sissy-Families®. After all sharing sex partners leads to **Sissy-Bonding**® [2.B2.13]. And as Jizz-Us® professed, this leads to a greater Sex-Spiritualism, erotic wholesomeness and profitable more morally uplifted America.

Wow! Father! I get aroused just listening to you profess the word of our God-of-Cocks! Ummm... Mwah... I know exactly what you mean. Sure, I can uplift my tits with a push-up bra, but how can we uplift the Sexual desires of the flock her at Church?

Exactly, my faith follower. Mwah... For example that Whore of a **SIT**® husband of yours. He's about as uplifted as a limp dick after an orgasm.

Yes! I know! But Sam Antha has a strong faith in our **Cock-God**®. My husband Sammy gets really nervous about his femininity. And Father, he is a dick-loving possessive boy-bitch for sure! Once he latches on to a nice big hard dick, he won't let go. He just starts kissing the man's erection.

Yes, yes, Mrs. Goldberg, I noticed after Cum-Union on Tuesday nights his obsession with being the first one to get my ordained penis in his mouth after I pull out of Jane's Vaganus®. He just needs to clean my dick of all the precious sticky Sissy-Poop® and Holy Man-Cream®.

Well Father Tom, despite his little cock hording game he plays, believe me, I'm the one wearing the skirt in our family. Don't worry I got my sinful bitch on a short leash.

Good, good, this is the Churches prescribed way to deal with a human **SIT**® Gurly-Boy like Samantha.

Yeah Father! I keep my **Sissy**® husband or should I call him my Bitch trained. I need his pay-check to manage our families budget. When he gets out-of-line I just give him a nice long hardcore rough ass rimming with an enormous strap-on. I bang him till his ass-pussy bleeds. Father he knows who the boss is. Huh! He thinks twice before misbehaving.

Very good Mrs. Goldberg. Mwah...

Oh please Father, I sooo wanna be your Bitch! Please call me your sinful Bitch. Mwah…

Well Sandy my dear! You're a Bitch-in-Heat of the HCC now that you've had the Sacrament of **Cum-Firmation**® [9.HS.6].

Yes Father. (Sandy reaches out and grabs Father Tom's boner which is obviously jutting out from his clerical cassock and hangs her head in reverence).

Sandy, I just wanted to tell you the two of you make a perfect Sissy® couple, you and your hot boy-bitch of a husband you have. And I've loved giving him the Sacrament of Penance by penetrating him in the blessed lovehole with my Holy-Cock®. Your **SIT**® husband is quite a hot little piece-of-ass.

But **Father** Tom, you know I don't wanna talk about Sam's skills. Yeah he's a cum guzzling, possessive, man-pleasing Whore®. But he's just a repenting Sissy who eats a girl-snatch and swallows Dick-Milk® better than a female bitch. What I really wanted to ask you is when are you gonna plow my sinful yet sweet backdoor Ass-Pussy, **HFA**® [4.D-G3.16] with your big wonderful ordained holy penis? Father I'm a sinner and I need you to administer penance to me with your hard boner!

Haaa... Haaa... Mwah…. Oh my dear **Sandy**! I would love to, but this depends on how many inches of repentance you are willing to accept. I can only administer my Holy-Cock® to the truly sinful girls.

Oooh **Father**! Please don't tease me! Don't play with me Father! You know I'm a Three-holer® kind of girl. Pick a hole your Holiness. Mwah… Ummm…

Mrs. Goldberg, **Sandy** you know only your SIT® husband can penetrate you in your Blessed Sissy-Making vagina! But, I'm more than ready to administer my penance by mount your sweet sinful poop-hole! Human Female Anus, your HFA hole. Heeee.... heee.... hee... Mwah... Kisss...

Yes certainly you're ready Father, you've been playing with your ordained holy prick for the last 69 minutes and by the way you're leaking pre-cum you're going to have to anoint a bitch with your Holy-Cream® very soon! Mwah... Mwah...

Mrs. Goldberg, would you like for me to anoint your HFA® bottom as I have done so many times before? Mwah... Kisss...

Oh Holy Cock-God! Yes... Kisss... Yes... Hold this thought and your hard dick Father Tom. First I have to go check on baby Jane. Seeing this much sperm leaking out of her cum-bucket little snatch means she might need to take a break soon and get douched-out. Kissss.... Be right back!

[4.6] LCB®

Sandy check on the LCB prayer bench...

Hey Mrs. **Goldberg**!

Hey **Johnnie**! How's my little lover Jane doing?

Jane's fine, but she's going to hit the limit soon for a one-year old **Sissy**®.

Oh yeah! How many has she taken so far?

Well she's had six and 6.9 ejaculations is the Orifice Safety and Health Administration, the **OSHA**® [23.34] limit.

Right! You're a good Spotter Johnnie. The federal protocol is they have to be douched-out every 6.9 cum loads.

Oh! And Mrs. Goldberg, don't forget the PrettyPuss® testing to assure a fresh clean Vaganus® orifice. Cock-God® she looks so beautiful!

Thanks Johnnie. Mwah… You sweet boy.

Yeah watching her in her Sissy-Baby® lingerie, those cute tiny platform shoes and taking it at both ends like a real Whore® she's just sooo adorable! Mrs. Goldberg I bet Jane is going to be a hot trap when she gets older. I'm hard for her!

Yeah for sure Johnnie! Jane is gonna empty a lot of nut-sacks. Mwah… (Sandy is running her hand over the Spotters crotch).

Huh! Mwah… (Johnnie smiles as his dick cums to attention). Mrs. G, I would mount her if I wasn't spotting for her.

Oh Johnnie it's obvious you would by the huge bulge in your pants (Sandy strokes him with her hand).

Yeah Mrs. G! Ahhh…

Well Johnnie you can have at our Sissy Jane anytime you want my friend, just cum on by for a feeding or sex training anytime. Our Whorehouse door is always open for a nice sweet young Stud® like you. And Johnnie, don't forget my ass-pussy is available for a second round if you're up for it.

Thanks Mrs. Goldberg, I'd gladly mount both of you for sure!

Okay! Cum here you little adorable lover **Gurl**®.

Mommy, mommy, cocky, cocky, cocky!

Okay, okay, let's get you cleaned-up nice and pretty. You're going to love the cleaning machine they have here in the ladies room, the **Douche-a-Matic**® 2500 [4.D-G1.*23*] is the best. Yeah, there you go. Oh! Wow! This is the best, better than the 1200 model we have at home.

Aaagh! Mommy! Mommy! Cummy! Ummm... (Jane smiles contentedly as she has multiple Sissygasms). Ahhh...

Haa haaa... Yes, baby Gurl®. Your little clit has Gurly cream shooting out! This douching machine does it all! It arouses you and cleans you all at the same time! It's so modern Jane.

Mommy I wov U! (Janie says in her little Gurly voice). I wov U Soooo much! Mwah...

Aaah! I love you too Honey-Bunny kisss... Now let's go back to the bench so you can make more men happy. Okay Honey-Bun?

Mommy! Mommy! Cocky! Cocky! Cocky! (Jane calls out for her favorite thing in the whole world).

Yes I know! I know, you want more men inside of you. Aren't they beautiful my Sissy-Baby? Big beautiful hard penises! Mommy knows what Jane Gurl® wants. Oh! And look at my eye-Phone® you made sooo much money for Mommy!

Here, you go Johnnie! She has a clean and fresh Sissy-Puss® and obviously ready to go at it again.

Thanks Mrs. G. I'll strap her in. Safety cums first.

Cocky, cocky, cocky! I want, I want... (Jane shouts).

Johnnie I can't get over how hungry Jane is.

Yeah Mrs. G, she craves having men more than any human female girl I've ever been with.

Well Johnnie the Sissification® drugs produced here in the United States at our National Sissification Laboratories are designed this way.

Right, right. When the Sissy parents take the drugs during the Sissy-Breeding® process, the Sissy fetus develops an unusual desire for penis. The result of the patented Sissy pregnancy is a non-human animal off-spring unlike anything in nature.

Yes Johnnie, Sissies are genetically modified to crave men. They be cum fully developed whores, much like the animals in nature. It's all part of building a new and more vibrant future here in America.

Ah huh! Mrs. G. our government has a plan to win the,

Race to the Bottom

We need to replace the non-productive middle working class with Sissy-Stud citizens. After all, it's a Whore-Pimp world we like in thanks to the Bankers.

Absolutely Johnnie! We're just eliminating our Cunt-tries liability. We import everything now, so we actually have no need for the middle, working Non-Stud population, just the wealthy 6.9 percent Aristocrat class on the top and the rest are Stud® pleasing Whores®. It's quite simple.

True Mrs. G. This is why our Law-Makers in Washingcum implemented the **RAT**© [23.47] economic theory. To get rid of the unneeded middle class, it's called the,

Rot-at-the-Top… !!!...

Yep! The **RAT**© economic theory was started back in the old Fascist days of the USA. Back in the Clitcum, Boosh, O-Bombs, Trump, the **CBOT**© era [21.B.5]. Back then, they started screwing the middle-class out of existence by sending jobs overseas and forced them into a debt-peonage.

True! And now hundreds of years later, here we are using the same Oligarchical contrived solution. Except nowadays we just starve them and enslave them in FEMA work-camps. But hey! Mrs. G, as long as we have **Vaganus**® and arousal medication in our lives, we'll have all the pleasure we need. We can just turn a blind-eye to all this political nonsense.

I agree Johnnie! And Pure Bred-Sissies like Jane will be there to provide orgasmic pleasure.

Yeah, yeah, as long as they're feed Man-Sperm from birth as their food source.

Oh yeah! So through nutrition, genetic mutation and sex training like we provide here at Church, they're naturally be cum attracted to the sexual pleasure provided by Stud® penetration.

Of course, Johnnie. They also have a biological instinct to feed on **Man-Cream**® as well. They develop an patented ad-Dick-tion to having penis in all their holes. Talking about holes, Johnnie I have to go take care of something. Mwah… See yah handsome! (Sandy, being in a hurry to get back to Father Tom, suggestively winks and blows a kiss at Johnnie).

See you Mrs. Goldberg! Thanks for the Sissy education talk and for the invite to your backdoor! See yah! (Johnnie blows a kiss back at Sandy).

Back to Father Tom…

Hey Father Tom! (Sandy cums skipping over). I see Samantha found you.

Yes, he, I mean she found me and intuitively went straight for my holy dick like a good little blessed Church Whore®.

Yeah He's my Sissy-husband! Always hungry for sex.

Guk… Gak…. (Sam slurping away on Father's fuckstick).

He is indeed Sandy! Aaaagh! He slurps on it like a faithful Whore! Aaaagh! Yeah! Suck it you cock worshipping boy-bitch! SLAP! (The Priest slaps Sam on the face hard)

Guk… Gak… Gek… Glrck… (Sam chokes on the shaft being forced down his throat).

Yeah bitch SLAP! Suck it! Holy Cock-God Sandy your husband sucks me like a true faithful follower.

Well Father Tom, before Sam Antha got in the Sissification® program he was just another pathetic unemployed middle-class loser like the rest of the 69 percent of this ass-backward Cunt-tree.

Huh! Then what happened?

Well, now look at him Father? Since he took-up the calling to worship the one true Cock, Jizz-Us®, he's turned his whole life around.

Amen! (Father shouts) Agh! Yeah Bitch! You better pray! (Says Father as he shoves his dick further down).

Sammy is in training, working a part-time job at a Whoring Station and has dignity and pride again. We just got lucky Father.

We're fortunate we live in the only Cunt-trie in the world who developed a Sissy-Stud culture.

Yes my child, Sissydom® is our salvation! Slap! Got lucky! Yes you did my dear that you did. There's only 6.9 percent of the population here in the United States Inc. which has been Sissified, Transmuted or Pure-Breed into Sissydom®. So there're still a lot of ordinary unemployed American males who were just misfortunate not to be selected to serve their Cunt-trie like Sam Antha was.

Guk… Gak… Gek… Glrck (Sam is on Sissy training meds to relieve the pain from all the disciplinary slapping).

Oh and my dear, don't forget all the prayers we've said for him here at The Blessed Sissy Lady of Cock-Whores.

Slurp, slurp… Slap! Glrck, Glrck…

Huh! I love slapping the shit out of your husband. Slap!

Well hit him harder Father, he needs to be disciplined. And yes, Father we are truly blessed, the HCC our Federal government, the wonderful Sissification drugs, I'm so proud to be a Cock worshiping American Sissy-Breeding® mother.

Amen! Praise Cock!

I think the drugs are great Father, especially the new SD69 prescription, it not only feminizes the males physically but also gets them to talk, and walk and act like real genuine girls.

Yeah! I know what you mean Sandy. Your Bitch-Husband moans like a girl, slurps and kisses like one. And it's amazing. Once Sammy started wearing women's cloths and putting on make-up I noticed I was getting hardons for the salvation of your boy-bitch husband.

[4.7] PENANCE

Ok! Ok! I'm good.

Slurp, slurp... Slap! Glrck, Glrck... (Sam follows his training and continues to slurp under any circumstance).

Samantha! I'm hard you can stop sucking me now.

Slurp... Slurp... I obey my man! (Sam shouts delirious from the medication).

Ok, you've done enough I said.

Glrck, Glrck... Guk... You're the man, I'm the Bitch! Guk...

Samantha! I said Stop! And I meant it!

Slurp... Kisss... Kisss... Slurp... I'm a man worshipping Bitch!

SLAP! SLAP! SLAP! Dam-it!

Ouch! (Father Tom slaps Samantha really hard in the face).

Yeah BITCH, when I say stop, you stop! I'm hard enough to bang your wife now! Bend-over my dear Sandy! I'm going to administer the Scared Sacrament of Penance® on you.

Oh Father, I offer my body to my Lord-of-Cocks in hope of my salvation.

Yes, I'm done face-fucking your man-craving sinful Sissy-husband. I'm going to slam my hard Holiness up your sinfully but beautiful, Cum-firmed Sissy mommy ass of yours. You're a sinner Sandy! Take it! Aaagh! (Father slams his prick into

Slap! Slap! (Father wants to score points with Sandy).

Yes Father! Thanks. Mwah... Slap my bitch he needs your Holy guidance. Oh thank you for doing me hard Father and absolving me of my sins.

Yes Sandy, my child, you are well cum. I've cleansed you of your sins against Studs for now.

Aaaagh! Yes! It was wonderful! Kisss... Kiss... Hmmm... lick... kiss. Yes, Father Tom hmm... kisss, you feel sooo good in me. So long and hard kiss kisss. I feel so cleansed and pure now, I'm so blessed! Sniffle, sniffle...

There, there, don't cry my child. You are a Blessed Sissy Mother who has been cleansed of her sins. There, there there's no need to cry.

Oh thank you Father, and knowing the cream you just gave me is Holy-Cream® and not just ordinary common non-blessed Stud Jizzies® like I get in our Whorehouse®. I feel free from sin now. Father, I'm so blessed!

Yes my dear child. Blessed art thou amongst Sissy breeding women and blessed is the fruit of thy whore womb. Now and at the hour of our orgasm. Amen.

Oh Father, kisss... Lick... Kissss. (Mrs. Goldberg bows her head in reverence and falls to her knees with tears rolling off her cheeks kissing repeatedly the Fathers dick head. Father Tom places his hands on Sandy's head), Oh Father, Kiss... Mwah...

Yes my child, worship the Holy-Cock® which has cleansed you of your sins. My child, all the faithful men of our parish have penetrated thy Blessed Cum-firmed ass-pussy. Sandy, you are so blessed to be the recipient of so many devout erect penises. You deserve all the sperm loads my dear Sandy.

Yes Father, we're so blessed, Samantha and I are both devoting our ass-pussies to serve as receptacles to the faithful of the HCC. We vow we'll pop-out as many Sissy babies as we can Father Tom. They will all be Baptized and Cum-firmed Sissy Whores here at the, Blessed Sissy Lady of Cock-Whores Church. They will always worship here Father Tom, I swear to you.

Good my dear child. We can never have enough religious Sissy Whore® Gurls to share our Holy-Cream with. And the Church appreciates your small financial donation from all the penetrations the Whores in your Sissy-Family receives.

[4.8] PSN

Father has another scheme for Sandy…

Well Sandy, after administering penance to you countless times, I got a hardon and started contemplating. As a man of the cloth, what can I do to make this poor horny child of the church more spiritually whole? And then it came to me like an epiphany! I want you to cum by my office in the church rectumory tomorrow in the afternoon.

Oh! Father Tom you want to hear my confession again?

No, well, yes I'd be glad to perform the Scared Sacrament of Penance on you again of course beside my balls will be bursting with a full load of Holy-Cream® by then.

Father! I'll do my penance right here in public! We don't have to hide in private anymore. All the Parishioners know I'm your Bitch!

Huh! Yes, yes Sandy, you being a slut is no secret. But what I really want to do is have a meeting with you and your Sissy husband Samantha about you possibly joining the, Holy Order of the Blessed Sisters of Priests or the HOBSOP. And take your vows to be cum a Priest Service Nun, a **PSN** [9.5].

Oooh My God! Oh Father! Are you sure I am worthy of this honor. (Sandy falls to her knees and kisses and licks Father Tom's huge male appendage) Huh! Me a Sister of a Priest? I should be that lucky to be a PSN! Father! You should be pissing on me. Everyone knows I'm a slut.

Oh my! Sandy yes, my dear I think you're very ready. Of course it will be difficult to pass all the tests to be cum a Nun to serve a Priest of the HCC. But I feel, it's obvious by the boner I have for you, you're ready for the challenge of serving a Priest.

Oh Father I'll do anything you ask of me! Mwah… Mwah… Ummm… Father (Sandy is all over him).

Yes, yes, down girl! I know you my child and this is why I will partition the Church for permission to allow you to be chosen as one of my Nuns. Sandy, are you ready to submit yourself to becoming one of the Nuns who serves me?

YES FATHER! YES! I'll be one of your Nuns. I'll obey you and do as you wish, (Sandy lustfully kisses the Fathers prick again) my Lord, your holiness I'll worship you Father.

Okay then, I'll see you tomorrow my dear and bring your bitch husband, you'll both need to sign some application forms.

Now go in the name of our Lord-of-Cocks and may peace be with you. Mwah…

Mwah… May peace be with you too. (Mrs. Goldberg bows her head in reverence as Father Tom leaves the room holding his empty nut-sack). Bye Father! (Sandy winks).

[4.9] RECTUMORY

Ding… Dong...

Good afternoon Father Tom. Mwah…

Mwah… Oh Sandy my dear, cum in and please drag your bitch in with you. (Sandy has Sam on a leash). Sandy just sign this application and then I'll have to have you remove (Father checks-out how scantily clad Sandy is). Wow, what little cloths you do have on off for a physical examination.

Oh and Sandy a relatively odd thing happen after I submitted the request for you to enter the Nunnery. I'm a little concerned.

Father! Is everything alright? Father I'll do anything to enter the convent, anything! I'll have as many orgasms as you wish my Lord!

Oh Sandy, you dear worshipper! Kiss... Yes your new mission in life is what you dream of having inside of you! Kiss... Mwah… Your promiscuous nature is obvious.

Sandy seriously, how well do you know your friend Mrs. Dune? And are the two, you know? Close friends? (Father winks). Like for instance, do you have play-dates and take off your cloths and such?

Oh well Father, Heather's my best friend! We were contacted by the Sissy Breed... Ahhhhh… (Sandy remembers the breeding Officials told her the Sissy-Bonding between Mary and Jane is a secret).

Oh and… Yeah, yeah, we're close Father. We do some intimate things of course, we're liberated type girls. I mean, we explore our girly parts. Do some smooching maybe, you know girl stuff.

Ah huh. (Father looks at Sandy with an inquisitive look). Sandy you were contacted by whom?

Nobody Father! Ahhhh…. We're really close me and Mrs. Dune.

Hmmm… Okay, well Sandy let me ask you this simple question, are Jane and Mary a Bonded Sissy Pair?

Ooooh Father! I shouldn't say anything.

Are the two of them a BSP? Tell the truth Sandy, you know the Cock-God is watching down on you (Father tries to play the god-card to scare Sandy into spilling the beans).

I have no idea what you're talking about Father! (Sandy un-buttons her blouse to distract the clergymen with temptation).

Haaa haa… Sandy my Dear, you're sweating and shaking. It's obvious you're not answering my question.

But Father I'm having a hot-flash for you (Sandy props up her huge tits with both hands and literally points her lactating nipples towards Father Tom).

Wow! Listen to me my dear Sandy. (Father looks at her with a stern look on his face). I know you were told to deny everything about what the Sissy Breeding Program, **SBP**® [4.D-G2.3] told you to do to your children.

I, I, I Father… (Sandy has to pull out all the stops and pulls hard on her blouse popping off the rest of the buttons. Then bats her eye lashes in a seductive manner in hopes of stimulating Father's libido will take over).

Haaa haa… Seriously Sandy? Huh! (The Father takes sandy in his arms to calm her down) Mwah… There's nothing to worry about. You can stop acting surprised.

Father, I'm a good Girl, I don't wanna be in trouble with you or Church.

Mwah… No worries. Mwah… Listen to me. Sissy® children are the property of our USA Inc. government. Sandy, you and Mrs. Dune are breeders and you do what you're told to do, like the good breeding whores you are. You were employed to breed livestock in your wombs. I mean for Love-of-Cock a veterinarian delivered your babies!

Am I a bad Girl Father? My tits lactate a lot when I get nervous. I sorry, I only wanted to breed a Sissy® so I could get a pay-check! And I'm pretty sure that's a sin!

Huh! It's okay! This is the life and times we live in. Believe me, our government is just as much a profiteer as you are.

Sniff… Sniffff…. I'm so ashamed of myself Father. Sniff…

Look Sandy, (Father looks Sandy in the eyes with an empathetic look). I don't know why Mary & Jane are of any importance to the **SBP**®. I've never seen them poking around like this. All I do know is, for whatever reason, these two Sissy Gurls® and you breeding mothers are of some special concern to our government. And this can mean only one thing.

What's that Father Tom? Sniff… Sniffff….

Ahhh… My guess is your Sissy® children are being groomed for the future of Sissydom®.

But Father why did the SBP® cum to you about it?

All I know is, this morning I was paid a visit. I was informed by these really intimidating government guys in black suites that, yes, you and Mrs. Dune are to enter the convent, complete your final vows of promiscuity and be returned to a life of servitude as Nuns. And under no circumstance is harm to cum to either of you or to your Sissy® children.

That was it? Okay. Father whatever it takes I'm all for it! Mwah… Mwah…

Mwah… Yes Sandy! Aghhh! Practice the faith of Cockolicism for the profit of our benevolent government and my Holy Ordained-Penis, Amen....

Aghhh! Father, protect me from evil! Mwah… (They're both half naked and almost to the bed where Sandy will gladly receive her penance).

Sandy, remember to make sure you and Heather enroll **Jane** and **Mary** into the Sissy Preschool here at the Blessed Sissy Lady of Cock-Whores church. The Gurls® have significance to the HCC.

Yes Father they are. And of course we will obey you. We want our children to have a strong faith in the Holy Cockolic Church.

Yes Sandy, your Sissy children will receive the guidance and training in Sissy Preschool necessary to propagate Sissydom® throughout the world.

Yes Father. We need to sacrifice our bodies to the Church.

Yes, yes… And if you really wanna get rid of your sins extra fast make sure a generous donation from all your Whorehouse® penetrations is forwarded to the Church. Amen.

For sure Father! And I'm sorry. Mwah… But why do we, the USA Inc. and the Holy Cockolic Church send Sissies to other Cunt-tries? I've always assumed we were trying to spread love & peace to the poor Sissy-less people.

Oh my dear Sandy! Well, yes, of course we're trying to help others and righteously so ourselves. You see, our American made Pure Breed Vaganus® have an ad-dick-tiveness.

Right! Like the old US Dollar did?

Correct my Child! Sandy, it's simple. If the United States Inc. has more Sexual-Power and money we can help ourselves which in turn, we may or may not help others depending on how profitable it is for us! The Cock-God would have wanted this.

Oh! Ahhh… Okay. (Sandy is just as confused as anyone else in the Cunt-trie by now and scratches her head).

Now don't worry your pretty little self over how many Sissies we sacrifice to save the world. Take the rest of your clothes off and let me make a thorough examine of your hot Sissy-Breeding body of yours! Hmmm.... Kiss.... Kisssss…. Mwah…

Continued in EN02, Chapter 1….

=== THE END ===

Review Request & Suggestion

Thanks for purchasing this book or bundle (four book set). Please leave a review on Google Books, Amazon or Audible. Also to help our readers or listeners, we strongly suggest downloading the Empty Nation manual **SM069** to assist with the complexity of the story from any one of the following.

Audible.com, free after purchase as a Product Summary

Amazon.com, (low price) ASIN: 1719912866

Google Play Books, (free) GGKEY: X02BGY24G4K

The Official Sissydom Manual SM069

The National Sissydom Association (NSA)
A subsidiary of USA Inc.
All rights reserved, copyright 2018
Revised: 11-01-2018

SM069-01 Description

The Sissydom manual version SM069-01 encompasses details from years 2213 to 2222. This manual is intended to be used by United States Inc. citizens for the sole purpose of clarification of the procedures, laws, rule, codes, regulations, probing, documents, exams, rating, ranking, classification, drugs, qualifications and behavior of all parties participating or remotely involved in the United States Inc. MSES (US-MSES).

TERRITORIES

This manual also applies to all occupied territories under control of the USA Inc. Including but not limited to all of Latin America (LA) including countries in both Central & South America; refer to the LA-MSES.

SAR

Special Administrative Regions (SARs) enjoy a higher degree of autonomy under the, One Cock World Order, **OCWO** [9.B.1] concept developed by Presidents Trump-Tramp-Dump. There are currently two SARs, Mexico located in the Central America and Canada in North America. Both were turned over to USA Inc. control after the NAFTA War in 2169. Both SARs mentioned here implement the LCT system.

Persons living in a SAR are NOT and never will be citizens of the USA Inc. Also neither is allowed to cross into the USA Inc. at any time (visas are not available) unless the border-crossing is for a female surrendering her rights and be cums a host-mother at a Sissy Farm Breeding facility.

MSES AFFILIATES

Although the following Cunt-Tries are not controlled territories or SARs of the USA Inc. they are dependent and liable to the USA Inc. monetarily. This pretty much means, the USA Inc. can squeeze their balls at any time to induce compliance.

IN-MSES (India)
RU-MSES (Russia)
IS-MSES (Islamic)
AU-MSES (Africa Union)
SE-MSES (Southeast Asia)

These Cunt-Trees are all implementing the MSES LCT system of payment (aka the new SWIFT system). For local rules and regulations consult the specific sections in this manual (section not available yet).

RULES

The rules and laws stated in this document are lawful and can be used in a court of law to defend and protect only the rights of United States of America Incorporated citizens. The USA Inc. governing body (Government) and any and all of its proxies or entities, owned, contained, endowed, funded, imprisoned, underwritten, confiscated, authorized, financed, detained, sanctioned, annexed, blockchained, begotten, empowered, captured, incorporated, forfeited, convicted, subjugated, forsaken, subsidized, sponsored, abandoned, franchised, promoted, controlled, conquered, incarcerated, entitled or restrained by said Government or its affiliated corporate members are fully relieved of any and all liability of wrong doing created by adhering to the laws, rules and regulations stated here in this SM069-01 document. Amen.

Please download the current manual SM069 for further details in Series…

About the Author Sue Yan Nish

Empty Nation Series published by What Is It Press. As far as the author of the series is concerned, we know very little about the Sue Yan Nish. We think she is a Chinese-American and lives somewhere in China. And although her location changes frequently, we receive cryptic messages form her. The messages simply tell us only that the manuscript is finished and where we need to retrieve it from. We leave her compensation in a small box and in the same place the manuscript was left for us.

Words from the Author

Hi my name is Sue Yan Nish.

My publisher What Is It Press asked me to write a little history about myself,

Here goes…

My father is an American, his name is, Dick Nish.

My mom is Chinese and her name is, Yan Liu Jiu. I was born on June 9th

They meet when my dad was working here in Chinese for the US State Department.

I live a simple and blissful life here in China. I love both of my parents and I'm not married. I finished college here in Shanghai, my major was Political Science with a minor in English.

I'm 26 years, 6 months 9 days old and NO I don't have a vaganus!

Common questions from my editor Sebastian De Angelis, which he asks me all the time, why don't I want publicity? And it really cum down to staying alive. We live in hostile times, government spying, people lurking in the shadows. I personally feel safer without the publicity, so yeah, I'm not reveling who I really am or where I am.

Another question frequently asked, if I live in China, how cum I know so much about the United States? My dad works for the State Department, need I say more!

Another question often asked, have I travel outside of China, the answer is yes, many times. I did cum-munity College in Hawaii. Traveled around the US visiting my Dad's family. Lived in San Francisco, Portland, and New York for a bit.

Author Contact Info

The following addresses are ways to get in touch with the author Sue Yan Nish.

Author Bio:
https://www.amazon.com/Sue-Yan Nish/e/B07GW252V1

Emails:
sueyannish@outlook.com
sueyannish@gmail.com

Website:
https://sites.google.com/view/empty-nation/home